Mandy and the Missouri Man

Linda Ford

Heartsong Presents

This story is part of a series about sisters. Sisters are special people with whom we share dreams and memories, hopes and frustrations. This story is dedicated to my sister, Leona, who is precious to me for providing that and so much more; for listening when I need to vent, for sharing prayer concerns and for being, most of all, my sister.

A note from the Author:

I love to hear from my readers! You may correspond with me by writing:

Linda Ford
Author Relations
P.O. Box 9048
Buffalo, NY 14240-9048

ISBN-13: 978-0-373-48614-4

MANDY AND THE MISSOURI MAN

This edition issued by special arrangement with Barbour Publishing, Inc., 1810 Barbour Drive, Uhrichsville, Ohio, U.S.A.

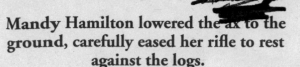

Mandy Hamilton lowered the ax to the ground, carefully eased her rifle to rest against the logs.

"Mister, them are fighting words. That's not the first time you've offended me. How do you propose to give me the satisfaction of justice?"

Trace Owens rolled his eyes at her drama. "What? You want a duel? Swords at sunrise? Pistols at noon?" He snorted.

A muffled giggle came from the tent where Cora listened to everything.

Mandy's gaze shifted that direction, filled with curiosity, then returned to him, as harsh as before. "I demand satisfaction."

Trace shook his head back and forth. "No way I'm fighting a girl."

She sputtered. "I'm as good as any man."

"At what?"

"Everything."

He simply stared at her. "I can't believe we're having this discussion."

Another muffled giggle from the tent. No doubt Cora was enjoying her brother's discomfort at being challenged by a woman.

Mandy stared toward Cora's hiding place. "Your wife?"

"My sister, and I'll thank you to stay away from her."

"I'll thank you to stay away from her." She mocked him. "I saw her from up the hill yesterday. She looked perfectly ordinary to me. What are you trying to hide?"

"Mind your own business."

LINDA FORD

and her husband raised a family of fourteen children, ten adopted, providing her plenty of opportunity to experience God's love and faithfulness. One of her goals in writing is to reveal a little of God's wondrous love through the lives of the people in her stories. She lives in Alberta, Canada, on a ranch she shares with her husband, a paraplegic client, boomerang children, and adorable visiting grandchildren.

Books by Linda Ford

HEARTSONG PRESENTS

Chapter 1

Mandy Hamilton squatted down on her haunches in the shadows and stared at the intruder invading her bit of land. No, she didn't have a deed saying it was hers, but it was the site she'd chosen. She had a secret ritual she did no matter where she lived. She found the best spot to build a home and in her imagination created a house for her family to live in…her sisters and their pa. A place where they would finally be together, safe and secure.

This man had no right to pitch his tent in the sunny little clearing nor build a campfire where she pictured the front step. Somehow she must convince him to leave. "It's mine," she whispered, as she slipped away as silent as the shadows hiding her, knowing he hadn't noticed her presence.

Soundlessly, she circled the area until she reached a

slight hill where she could operate without fear of discovery. Again she settled on her haunches—a position she had grown to prefer. It allowed her to gain her feet quickly yet provided relative comfort as she studied whatever she desired to watch. Wearing trousers made the position easy to maintain. There were those who frowned on her wearing them, but she'd long ago learned they made life in the woods a lot easier. She pushed up the sleeves of her white shirt to cool her arms and settled back to watch. The man tramped about the clearing as if measuring it. Like he thought he owned it. Nothing had been said around town about someone filing claim on any land in the area so she guessed he was only a squatter.

On *her* land.

If her gaze could cross the distance she would fry him in his tracks, but all she could do was narrow her eyes and stare.

If she had anything to say about it, he'd soon change his mind about thinking he owned the land.

She pressed deeper into the shadows, lifted her head to bark and howl like a wolf—many wolves. All the while she kept her attention on the man below. He jerked toward the sound, and she grinned with satisfaction. All those hours prowling the woods had taught her many valuable skills, but she'd never imagined imitating a wolf would come in so handy.

Moving quickly to the left, she climbed higher and repeated wolf sounds as if animals circled the clearing.

The man strode toward the tent and snagged up a rifle then headed straight toward her. His wide-brimmed hat sat low on his forehead so she couldn't see much of his face, but the set of his jaw informed her he meant to put an end to any threat from a marauding pack of wolves.

She didn't intend to wait to see what he'd do if he realized he'd been duped by a woman. Fact is, she didn't intend he should find out. If she could convince him wild animals objected to his presence, making it an unsafe place, then she would have accomplished what she set out to do.

Soundlessly, she slid away before he neared her location.

A few minutes later, she sank down in another place and waited, watching his shape slip through the trees. For a time he disappeared and she tensed, hoping he wouldn't shoot willy-nilly into the bushes. But in a bit she detected him returning to the camp. He was almost as quick and silent as she was. She allowed herself a fleeting moment of admiration then dismissed it. Neither stealth nor skill mattered. He didn't belong here.

He reached the open and studied his surroundings. She didn't move, knowing she was invisible among the trees. He removed his hat and brushed back a mop of dark blond hair. She took the opportunity to assess him further. From what she could determine at this distance, she guessed he was close to her age. She'd seen every sort of man go through the Bonners Ferry Stopping House. Every shape and size, so she eyed this one up with a practiced look. He wore a yoked western shirt, such as she'd seen on bow-legged cowboys passing through. He looked solid. Muscular. Like a man who worked for a living rather than push a pen across paper. Probably a man seeking gold. But then why was he in her clearing? Shouldn't he be headed for the ferry and the gold fields to the north?

He jammed his hat back on his head, cradled the rifle in his arms, and returned to pacing out the clearing.

She again climbed the hill and made wolf calls, grinning at the way the man jerked toward the sound. She moved away. Should the man decide to fire blindly toward the source, she didn't intend to be within range. A few minutes later she leaned against a tree to observe the clearing.

A movement at the tent caught her attention, and her mouth fell open. Someone was inside. And it wasn't the man she'd tried to scare off. She sought his figure just to make sure, but he'd disappeared. She rubbed her eyes and stared. Had he moved into the tent so quickly she'd missed it? Impossible.

The person in the tent inched out far enough for Mandy to see it was a woman. Or a girl, who clutched a poke bonnet to her cheek and hunched her shoulders forward. Someone ought to warn her about bad posture. The girl—or woman, if she be that old—seemed afraid. At least, that was how Mandy read her furtive movements as she jerked little peeks about her then retreated into her rolled forward shoulders.

Mandy hadn't had something so interesting to watch for a long time. She sat back again to observe.

"You stay out of sight while I take care of this," twenty-year-old Trace Owens told his sister. It was no wolf harassing him. At least not the four-legged kind. He knew plenty of the two-legged variety. Could his treacherous associates have followed him here? He'd seen no sign of them in weeks. But whoever it was would soon discover Trace had no patience left for people bothering them. He'd run so far he felt like a foreigner in his own country. Seemed this distant corner of America was not involved with the civil war. He hoped it was true.

He cast a glance over his shoulder to the clearing. This little spot—a pleasant distance from the nearest town of Bonners Ferry—suited him just fine, and he wouldn't be harassed away by some mischief-making person.

It would take more than a fake wolf to drive him onward. But he prayed to God they'd outrun the dogging threat of troublemakers. Not that he prayed much anymore. Didn't seem to be any use in it. Except for Cora's sake.

He'd listened to the wolf call as the person circled the camp. Knew whoever did it would move away, figuring Trace would go toward the sound. He went the opposite direction, moving silently among the trees, pausing often to listen for any rustle to indicate movement.

His opponent was good—he'd give him that. But after a bit he was rewarded with the sound of a little gasp. He wondered what caused it but didn't let curiosity distract him. He focused on the sound and edged closer.

There he was. Squatted down, looking toward the clearing. Trace wondered what held his attention so completely but didn't shift his concentration as he narrowed the distance between them.

He was close enough now to spring, and he did, bowling the spy over and pressing his slight frame to the ground. Their hats fell off, and he looked into the face of—

A woman! In man's trousers!

A woman with a thick, untidy braid of dark brown hair and dark brown eyes that widened in surprise then narrowed, filling with anger and purpose.

He realized his peril just in time and clamped her hands to the ground beside her head. He kept her body weighed down so she couldn't kick or hit or…

He jerked back as she reared her head, intending to do damage to Trace's face. Did she realize it would hurt her as much as him?

She bared her teeth and flung about, trying to get a mouthful of flesh.

He leaned back as far as possible while still restraining her. "Why are you spying on me? Pretending to be a wild animal?" He snorted. "Guess it isn't much of a pretense. You *are* a little wild animal."

That certainly did nothing toward calming her. She kicked and reared and flung her head some more.

He tightened his hold. "Answer the question. Who are you, and what do you want?"

Lifting her head, she gave him a look that practically peeled the skin from his face. "Get off me."

He considered his options. If he let her go, she'd either run away or attack him. He intended to find out why she was spying on him before he let her escape. But he had no desire to be the target of her feet and fists and teeth and goodness knows what else if he released her. Likely a knife and certainly a gun, though he saw her rifle had been kicked aside in the scuffle.

She followed the direction of his gaze, but the distant rifle did nothing to mellow her. "Let me go." After a few minutes fighting to escape him, she grew still. "I have never been treated this way by a man. And I will exact justice."

"I didn't know you were a woman." Still he didn't move, knowing once freed she posed a risk to his safety.

"Well, I am. And now you know."

Yes, now he knew. That didn't make her any less dangerous. But he couldn't stay where he was. It was indecent. He clamped both her wrists in one hand and leaped to his feet. Just as he guessed, she kicked and twisted and fought. But he held on. Not until she told him why she spied on them would he let her go. He repeated his questions.

"I could ask the same of you." She spat the words out in between jerks and twists.

"Fine. I'm—" Did he want his name known? Not that it wasn't a good name. Why, his father had been a hero in the Mexican-American War, which was the cause of all their trouble. But he'd lost enough. He wasn't going to lose his name, too. "I'm Trace Owens."

"What are you doing here?"

"You mean besides trying to calm you down?" He panted from the effort of restraining her.

"Sure picked a strange way of doing it." She swung her foot and connected with his knee.

He grunted. At least she wore moccasins, not hard boots. He might survive a kick or two.

"I aim to build me a house and live here." Fighting with her had deepened his consideration into determination.

"Yeah." She twisted full circle, forcing his hands to burn a ring around her wrists. "You own the land? Got a deed to it?"

"Nope. Figure building a house makes it mine." He'd see about filing on the land after he got settled. Didn't seem to be any rush to go into town for the task. The longer he kept his presence a secret the better he'd feel.

The kick she aimed at him was meant to do serious damage. He managed to jump aside and still hold her wrists.

"You can't have the land. It's mine."

He hadn't considered someone might own the property. "You got a deed?"

"No. Don't need one."

"Neither do I." He jerked her wrists upward, forcing her to stand on tiptoes, effectively making it impossible for her to kick or bite. He realized she was almost too tall for him to be able to do so. Tall and tough. Bold and beautiful. "What's your name?"

"I ain't telling."

"Expect I could go to town and ask. Maybe tell everyone about this little incident."

She looked about ready to spit. "It's Mandy Hamilton. Not that it's any of your business."

"Suppose not. But seems we both figure we got a claim to the same piece of land." He lowered her slightly, as much to ease his arms as hers, and leaned in closer, hoping she wouldn't break his nose with a head bunt. "Seems the one who builds a house first is the rightful owner, and that will be me."

He was ready for her explosion but even so it was all he could do to hold her at arm's length. He'd long ago started to sweat from the effort. Beads of moisture dripped from his forehead. He bent to wipe his face on his sleeve.

She took advantage of the movement to jerk back hard enough to make him stagger forward, close enough for her to bring her knee into his middle. He groaned but held on. Would she buy his declaration that building a house established a claim? Or would she only pretend to and head off to town to file on the land?

"Mister, that's my land. I saw it first, and I aim to keep it. You won't find it easy to build a house there. I'll see to it."

He straightened, forced her to face him. "Lady, I'm claiming that land. See, I already live there." He twisted to glance at his tent and the horses tethered a distance away. "It's mine." Cora peered from the tent flap, watching the tussle. He couldn't see her face but knew she'd be frightened. They'd both hoped they could find seclusion here. This feisty woman could make that dream an impossibility. Maybe he could bargain with her. "What would it take to persuade you to leave us alone?"

Another look that made him fear for his safety. "What would it take to persuade *you* to get off *my* land?"

So that's the way she meant to be? So be it. She wasn't the first challenge he'd faced nor likely would she be the last.

He tossed her arms free.

She rubbed her wrists and favored him with a dark scowl.

"Have it your way." He jammed his fists to his hips. "Turn this into a fight, but I won't be driven off. Seems to me whoever is living here and building a house would be declared the official owner." He didn't know if the law would support him in that claim, but it seemed reasonable.

"Fine. You want a fight, mister, you've got a fight. But I intend to fight fair." The look on her face made him wonder what she meant. "First one to build a house and live in it gets the land. Agreed?" She stuck out her hand.

He drew back, expecting her to engage in another tussle.

She shoved her hand closer. "You willing to shake on it?"

"Agreed." He was ready for the way she squeezed his hand and squeezed back equally hard.

She jerked free and strode away, chin in the air.

He stared for a moment then chuckled. With her baggy trousers and overly big shirt it was no wonder he'd thought her a man at first glance. But she was most certainly a woman. And he didn't have to wrestle her to the ground to know it. She had a face of unusual beauty.

She moved with stealth and disappeared into the woods like a shy deer.

He snorted. Mandy Hamilton was no shy deer. More like the wolves she imitated.

How much risk did she pose? Could he trust her to

keep their presence quiet? Not likely. He did not intend to trust anyone for anything from now on.

First one to build a house owned the land, she said. Who could say if she meant it or only meant to trick him? But if he had a house built, he would have a reason to dispute anyone filing on the land.

He jogged down the hill to his campsite.

Cora stepped into the sunshine. "Who was that?"

"Nobody. You'll be okay. But I got to hurry and start a house."

"So we're staying here?" She glanced about as if taking real stock of her surroundings.

"It's a fine place. We'll be safe here."

She sighed. "Already one person has found us. How soon until more come to stare?" She pulled her bonnet closer to her cheek.

He hesitated, caught between the urgency of getting trees chopped down and trimmed for a house and the sad note in his sixteen-year-old sister's voice. Cora's need won out. He went to her side. "Cora, baby sister, you are still a beautiful girl." With a great deal of self-control, he stilled the anger souring his insides. The treachery of people he'd once trusted brought them to this place and made his sister endure her disfigurement.

She pushed her bonnet to her shoulders and faced him full on. "So long as you don't look too closely."

He'd learned not to flinch at the sight of the scars on the side of her face, but it never failed to sear his insides. He touched her shoulder. "You're lucky to be alive." He'd do all in his power to protect her from prying eyes. But how was he to keep Miss Hamilton away?

Emotions worked across Cora's expression—anger, sorrow, denial, and finally, resignation. "I suppose some would think so." The flatness of her tone denied the truth of her words.

No need to agree or disagree on the subject. He knew she didn't count herself lucky. Often enough she'd said she wished she'd died in the fire along with their parents. No amount of reassurance on his part changed her mind. He seemed the only one happy that she'd lived.

"I just wish people would leave us alone."

He hated the harsh tone of her voice and hoped changing the subject would lighten her mood. "The house I'm going to build will be small to begin with, but it will be warm and dry and better than sleeping on the ground under dank canvas."

She sighed. "I suppose so."

"Do you want to come with me into the woods? I'm going to start cutting down trees."

She looked wistful, and for a moment he thought she might agree. Then she shook her head. "I'll stay here."

"You'll be okay by yourself?"

"You won't go far, will you?"

He thought of what he'd seen in his earlier scouting trips. Seemed there might be enough suitable trees within shouting distance to start with. "You'll be able to hear me working."

"Then I'll sit here and read."

He hated to leave her. Anytime she said she'd read he figured she mostly stared into space, but he had to get a house started if he meant to beat Miss Hamilton. "I'll be back before dark. If you need me, just come or call out." He grabbed his ax and headed for the woods.

Mandy fumed all the way back to Bonners Ferry then pulled up hard. If she steamed into the stopping house, Joanna would start asking all sorts of questions. Joanna could get very nosy. Four years her senior, Joanna had been the mother figure for both Glory and herself since their ma died eight years ago. Joanna had only been fourteen at the time, and she'd done a good job of taking care of them. But she took her responsibilities very seriously. And heaven forbid she would encounter her other sister. Ever since Glory had fallen in love with the preacher man, Levi, why, Glory had been too high and mighty for her own good. As if she had figured out the answer to all life's problems just because she'd succumbed to love.

A couple of times, Mandy had challenged her to an Indian wrestle, but Glory only laughed and said, "Poor Mandy."

Mandy ground about and headed up the hill away from *her* place. She needed to think and plan. That miserable cur of a man thought he could claim her land, did he? Well, she'd show him he didn't stand a chance against her.

A part of her brain mocked. Yup, you showed him good who was boss, didn't you? He had you sprawled helplessly on the ground. Then practically hung you from his hands.

She admitted with some reluctance that it took a mighty big man to lift her to her tiptoes. Mandy Hamilton was tall and had more muscle per inch of body than half the men she'd met, and she'd met plenty. Her insides burned with humiliation at the way the man had roughhoused her. She forced that insult aside to contemplate the urgency of building a house. She plunked to the ground to consider the quandary the man had forced upon her.

No time for a real house, even though her dreams included a tidy little dwelling with at least two bedrooms, a kitchen and a front room, and a stoop big enough to hold buckets, shovels, and a supply of wood.

She smiled. A stoop would serve as a cabin for now.

No one said it had to be fancy. Just a place to live. That's all she needed to gain ownership of the land. Of course, she could walk down to the lawyer's office and fill out a claim, but it didn't sound like half as much fun as beating the man at a challenge.

A frown drew her mouth down. She needed to beat him to salve her pride.

A little later she sashayed into the stopping house with several dressed grouse for tomorrow's meal.

Joanna glanced up. "I was beginning to think you got yourself lost."

Mandy chuckled. "When was the last time I got lost?"

Joanna grinned. "So long ago I can't remember. Glory seems to have disappeared though."

The sisters looked at each other and sighed.

"No doubt helping Levi put up his mission house," Mandy said unnecessarily. Both knew where she was and why.

"Says they won't marry until the place is finished." Joanna giggled. "Seems she's in a big hurry to get hitched."

They both had a good laugh and then sobered.

"It won't be the same without her," Mandy said.

Joanna hugged Mandy then broke away. "We still have each other."

Mandy developed a sudden interest in the array of pies on the table. What would Joanna do if Mandy built a house and moved into it? But it wasn't as if she planned to stay there day and night. She'd still provide food for the stopping house and come every day to help. "You need anything done?"

"You could haul out the ashes, fill the wood box, and sweep the lean-to floor before people start arriving."

As she did the chores, Mandy planned her house.

Chapter 2

Mandy hurried through her morning chores at the stopping house then called, "I'll be back later."

Joanna waved her away. Nothing unusual about Mandy's announcement. Almost every day she went hunting, keeping the place supplied with fresh meat. But today she swung her rifle over her shoulder and detoured by the woodshed to pick up the ax. On second thought… She took a few steps away and then backtracked… . She would take along a hammer and nails, too.

Glory had chosen the moment to get an armload of wood. She stared. "You're going hunting with an ax?"

"Aren't you supposed to be helping Levi?"

"He's ordering supplies. I'm going up there later." The way she eyed the ax, Mandy knew even mention of Levi hadn't distracted her.

"You're letting him order supplies on his own?" She

hoped the doubt in her voice would trigger concern in Glory and send her after Levi.

"I think he can manage. What kind of animal do you hunt with an ax?" Her eyes narrowed. "You aren't going to go into hand-to-hand combat with a bear, are you?"

Mandy laughed. "I might."

Glory snorted. "Even you aren't that stupid."

"You calling me stupid?"

Glory shrugged. "I'm not going to fight with you."

"Cluck, cluck." Mandy made flapping motions with one arm, the other otherwise occupied with holding the ax.

Glory simply shrugged again. "You can't provoke me today. I'm in too good a mood."

"Well, ain't that sweet?"

"Unlike you, who seems determined to be miserable."

"Am not." Didn't take any effort at all to be grumpy with an intruder on her land. She strode away.

"So where are you going with the ax?" Glory fell in at her side.

"You sure are hard to figure out, Glory. When Joanna needs you to help, you can't be found anywhere—"

"I can always be found helping Levi."

"Then when I have something to do that I don't need help with, you stick to me like a bad smell."

Glory punched her shoulder. "I don't smell. At least, not bad."

When Mandy ignored Glory's attempt to start a tussle, Glory deliberately bumped into her, making her sidestep off the path.

"Stop it."

"Tell me where you're going with the ax."

Mandy drew to a halt and faced her sister. Glory was a year older and a daredevil who liked to ride wild horses and challenge any man who abused his animals. Did Levi have any idea what he was getting himself into by marrying Glory? She sighed. Her persistent sister would not give her any peace until she found out what Mandy intended with the ax. "If you must know, I'm going to build a house."

Glory roared with laughter then seeing Mandy's frown, sobered. "You're serious, aren't you?"

"I've always wanted a house."

"Yeah. And no doubt you think Pa will come and live with you, and you'll be a happy family at last."

"So what if I do? I don't hate Pa like you do. I wish he would come back."

Glory lifted her hands in a sign of defeat. "I don't hate Pa. I just don't have any expectations of him. I no longer hope and pray he'll come back and make a home for us. Besides, in case you've forgotten, I'm going to make a home with Levi. He'll never walk out on me the way Pa always does."

Mandy kept her mouth clamped shut. They'd had this argument before.

"You don't need Pa anymore either. We're all independent, full-grown women now."

Mandy hurried away.

Glory followed.

"I guess it's too much to hope you might leave me alone."

Glory ignored Mandy's dig. "Where are you going to build this house?"

"I got a place picked out."

"Oh yes. I remember. Every time we move, you pick out the place where we will suddenly become a happy family with Pa living contentedly with us."

Mandy didn't slow down. Not that it discouraged Glory.

"So where is this place you got picked out?"

"If I tell you, will you drop the subject?"

"Maybe."

Mandy stopped, pointed up the valley. "On that hill over there. A nice flat clearing with hills rising on one side."

While Glory studied the place Mandy pointed out, Mandy resumed her journey.

Glory hurried after her.

Mandy sighed loudly.

"You've always had this dream but never before built a house. Why now? Is it because I'm getting married? Does that make you feel like our family is falling apart even more than Pa leaving all the time? Because I'm not leaving. I'll be real close. You'll probably get downright tired of me being so close."

Mandy ground to a halt and stared at Glory. "Are you out of your mind? This has nothing to do with you." A blast of exasperation exploded from her lungs, and she lifted a hand in defeat and amazement. "If you must know, it's because someone else thinks they can own my land. If I build a house first, it will be mine."

"Why don't you just file on it?"

"Because…" It made perfect sense, but completely eliminated any possibility of besting the man. "I intend to claim it fair and square by getting my house up first."

"What do you know about building anything? Seems to me any time that kind of work came up you disappeared."

"Someone had to find food."

"Yeah, but using a rifle isn't a skill that will help you build a house."

"How hard can it be?" She steamed onward, Glory sticking to her side like a burr.

"Who is this person who wants your land? A man, I assume."

"A man by the name of Trace Owens."

"So you've met him?"

Mandy's insides flared hot at the memory.

"Is he alone or does he have a family?"

Mandy jerked to a halt so fast that Glory had to retrace her steps. "There was someone. A woman or girl, I couldn't be certain."

Glory tapped her chin and considered this newest bit of information. "Did you ever think he might need the land more than you do?"

It was enough to make Mandy want to wrestle Glory to the ground until she hollered stop. "Look around you." She waved her arm in a wide circle. "There's plenty of other places." She pushed past her sister and hurried down the trail. "Let him find something else."

After a bit she realized Glory hadn't followed. About time. She went directly toward the clearing where she would build her house.

Trace swung his ax again and again, the shudder racing up his arm a constant reminder of his despair. No point in crying over spilled milk, as Ma would say.

He lowered the ax to the ground and bent over, moaning as pain with no physical cause clenched his innards.

Bad enough Ma and Pa had died. But the reason, the treachery behind it. Behind Cora's scars…

He lifted the ax and attacked the tree, welcoming the ache in his limbs from the hours he'd devoted to this kind of work.

But pain in his body did not neutralize the pain in his heart.

He knew nothing would. Not time. Not drink. Nothing but death, and he was too stubborn, too proud to let his enemies drive him to that. Besides, what would happen to Cora if he weren't around to care for her?

The tree fell, and he set to peeling it, sweat pouring from his brow and soaking his shirt.

No one would drive him from this place. Certainly not a woman who could pass for a man. A grin skated across his lips. No way could he be fooled into thinking she was a man. Not with those full lips, wide eyes, and feminine body.

The ax slipped, but he caught it before he did himself damage. He needed to focus.

No man or woman was driving him away. He was through running. And hoped they were far enough from his past that no one would bother them.

He secured a chain to the logs, attached it to the horse, and dragged them to the camp.

There she was. Mandy Hamilton. Complete with ax and rifle and, if he wasn't mistaken, a hammer in the pocket of her baggy pants. She circled the logs he'd already placed.

She turned a jaundiced gaze toward him as he drove the horse close to the house. "See you've been hard at work."

"You'll never catch up."

"Sounds surprisingly like a dare."

He grunted. Seems they'd already established it was a competition, at the very least. "What's to stop either of us from going to the land title office and putting our name on the deed legal-like?"

Her look shot daggers at him. "On my part, honor. I

said first one to build a house—and live in it—gets the land. When I say something, I do it. I keep my word."

The words came out like hot bullets. He wondered if she meant them as strongly as she spoke them. "I ain't got much use for words. Easily spoken. Easily forgotten or excused."

She lowered the ax to the ground, carefully eased her rifle to rest against the logs. "Mister, them are fighting words. That's not the first time you've offended me. How do you propose to give me the satisfaction of justice?"

He rolled his eyes at her drama. "What? You want a duel? Swords at sunrise? Pistols at noon?" He snorted.

A muffled giggle came from the tent where Cora listened to everything.

Mandy's gaze shifted that direction, filled with curiosity, then returned to him, as harsh as before. "I demand satisfaction."

Trace shook his head back and forth. "No way I'm fighting a girl."

She sputtered. "I'm as good as any man."

"At what?"

"Everything."

He simply stared at her. "I can't believe we're having this discussion."

Another muffled giggle from the tent. No doubt Cora was enjoying her brother's discomfort at being challenged by a woman.

Mandy stared toward Cora's hiding place. "Your wife?"

"My sister, and I'll thank you to stay away from her."

"I'll thank you to stay away from her." She mocked him. "I saw her from up the hill yesterday. She looked perfectly ordinary to me. What are you trying to hide?"

"Mind your own business."

Her eyes hardened. "Mister, you have offended me yet again. It's about time we dealt with this."

"Okay, fine. What do you have in mind? Another wrestling match like yesterday?" He grinned, letting her see just how much fun it had been to subdue her.

She blushed clear to her hair line. "A shooting match."

He chortled. "You're on."

They reached for their rifles in one fluid movement.

She cradled hers in the crook of her arm. "First, let's be clear about what's at stake."

"I'm sure you're going to tell me."

"Yup. You win, I forgive your insults. But when I win, which I will, you let me meet your sister."

They both heard the gasp from the tent.

"'Fraid that's not my call."

"Ask her if she's willing."

He could almost hear her asking if he was afraid. He was certainly not afraid of her. She was a woman. If he couldn't outshoot a woman, he better put on a dress and grow out his hair. "Cora, what do you think? You don't have to agree."

He waited, picturing the struggle his sister would be enduring.

"If I refuse it sounds like I don't think you'll win. But I know you will, so I agree."

"Done." Mandy held out her hand.

"Done." This ought to be fun. Like taking candy from a baby. Her firm hand in his reminded him he was not dealing with a helpless child.

They agreed on targets and took their places.

"Ladies first," he said generously. After all, he didn't want to intimidate her with his skill.

Her face hardened, and he sighed. He didn't need her

to step back and refuse to lift her rifle to know he'd be the one shooting first.

"Don't say you didn't ask for it." He lined up a bead.

Mandy stood back to watch. The man had loads of confidence. It showed in the way he widened his stance and pressed his cheek to the stock. It revealed itself in his assurance he could outshoot her. In fact, if they weren't in competition she might admire his self-assurance. He was going to need it. 'Cause she intended to beat him soundly.

He curled his finger around the trigger, and a shot rang out. The piece of wood serving as target exploded. Five more times without a miss. He lowered his rifle and stood back, grinning as if he'd already won the contest. "Ready to concede defeat?"

She flicked him the barest of glances. Defeat? He'd soon be crowing out the other side of his mouth. She knelt on one knee and rested her elbow on the other, eased her sights on the target, and squeezed off a shot. The chosen wooden target exploded. She reloaded five times, and five more targets followed suit. She rose and faced him. "Ready to concede defeat?"

"Not a chance." He glanced about, pointed out a dead tree branch a fair piece away. "I'll get that in the first shot."

"If you don't, I will." She indicated he should go ahead. He took his time lining it up then fired. At first she thought he missed, but then the branch cracked and fell to the ground. He was good. She'd give him that.

Just not good enough.

"See that branch?" She indicated one several yards past where he'd shot. "I'll take it down first shot."

He hooted disbelief. "Lady, if you do, I will concede defeat."

"Prepare to concede." She knelt again, studied her target, shifted when the sunlight glinted off the barrel. She pushed her hat back and steadied her arm, drew in her breath, held it, and squeezed very slowly. At this distance, she couldn't afford the least mistake. The rifle cracked. She pushed to her feet, her eyes never leaving the branch she'd aimed for. It exploded from the tree.

Ears ringing from so many shots, she bent enough to rest her rifle against the logs then turned to face Trace, a grin threatening to split her face in two.

His mouth hung open, and he stared toward the now-missing branch.

She whooped. "I win."

His attention jerked toward her. Admiration replaced surprise, albeit reluctant admiration. "That was a fantastic shot." His gaze held hers, exploring, she supposed, what kind of woman could shoot like that. Better than any man. But he continued looking at her, causing her insides to shift as though he offered something she hungered for.

How stupid. She didn't need anything. Especially from a man. Hadn't she proven over and over that she could manage without her pa, without any man? Hadn't all the Hamilton sisters?

She shifted her gaze and did a little victory dance up to him. "I won. I won. I won." She danced back to where she started. Only then did she face him again, wondering what she would see. No doubt anger, displeasure at being beaten by a woman.

But he grinned widely, his eyes flashing appreciation.

Her words died on her lips, and her feet ceased dancing. The only part of her body that still moved was her heart, and it rattled against her ribs like a trapped animal trying to escape.

"No one likes a sore winner," he groused, still grinning. His gaze trapped her. Then he glanced toward the tent, freeing her to suck in air and shake herself inside for being so easily affected by a smile. Like she was some sort of foolish female. She followed his gaze and waited.

"Cora." He sounded so regretful she almost backed down from their agreement. But curiosity overrode any weakness. What kind of woman hid in a tent?

"I know." The disembodied voice sounded uncertain, maybe even a little unsteady. "I can't believe you let a woman outshoot you."

"I can't believe it either," Trace said. "But she's awfully good."

Mandy faced him. "I tried to warn you." Whatever silly thing she'd felt must have been only fleeting foolishness. But then his gaze collided with hers, and her heart dipped like it had broken free from its hitching post. She jerked away. What was wrong with her? "I won fair and square."

"No argument with that. And we'll live up to our agreement. Won't we, Cora?"

"We're honorable people no matter what others might say."

That was a mighty peculiar observation, but before she had time to consider it, the tent opening flapped. His sister edged out, though she clung to the bit of canvas as if it served as an anchor. "Hello, I'm Mandy Hamilton. I'm pleased to meet you." If you could call this a meeting.

Cora hunched forward as she had the first time Mandy saw her. She pulled the poke bonnet close to her face. She didn't even bother to look at Mandy. Wouldn't allow Mandy to see her. A sting of sympathy caught Mandy's heart. "I know what it's like to be shy. I'm not much good around people myself. Kind of prefer being out in the woods watching the animals. Do you like animals?"

A brief nod acknowledged the question.

"I can move through the woods so quiet I can get right up to a deer. Maybe I could show you how."

The girl jerked toward her, allowing her a brief glimpse of her profile then turned away before Mandy could garner any details. From what she could see, the woman was barely out of childhood. "How old are you?"

"She's sixteen," Trace said.

"Can't she talk for herself?"

"'Course I can. I'm sixteen just like he says."

"I'm eighteen. Perhaps we could be friends. Apart from my sisters, I've not had a friend for a long time."

"Why not?" Cora asked.

"Mostly because we move around too much."

"Why do you move?"

"It's a long story. Sure you want to hear it?"

One shoulder lifted in a shrug. "I wouldn't mind."

"Very well." She sank cross-legged to the ground. "Our pa is always chasing off after one adventure or another. Ma and us girls would follow after him. Ma died eight years ago, but we still tried to keep up with him. Gotta tell you it wasn't always easy to track that man. He moved so frequently we were often two stops behind him. Guess if a man isn't interested in keeping his family together, he doesn't really have anything to keep his feet in one place. Pa's been everywhere, tried everything."

"Like what?"

Mandy shot a glance at Trace to see what he thought of this mostly one-sided conversation.

He smiled encouragement, and her heart again lurched inside her chest.

Hoping to save her heart further wear and tear, she shifted her attention back to Cora.

The girl didn't hunch quite as markedly. Guess she

was enjoying the storytelling, so Mandy continued. "He worked on building railroads, hunted wolves, hunted buffalo... ." She laughed a little. "Right now he's off hunting gold in the Kootenais."

"Why didn't you follow him there?"

"I wanted to, but Joanna—that's my eldest sister—she saw the chance to run the Bonners Ferry Stopping House. Said we could support ourselves nicely. Glory agreed, so I was outvoted."

"Who is Glory?"

Trace settled on the ground close by. She studied him, wondering if he'd had enough. He nodded. "Go on. This is the most she's talked to anyone but me in a long time."

"Glory is my sister. She's a year older." She paused.

The girl remained on her feet, her back to Mandy, her shoulders hunched. She must be getting uncomfortable.

"Cora, why don't you come over here and sit with us? I'll tell you more about Glory."

For answer, Cora ducked back inside the tent and pulled the flaps tight.

Mandy sought Trace's eyes, wanting to apologize. "I only wanted to make her welcome. Be a friend." Such sadness and regret filled his expression that her exuberant heart spasmed hard.

"Leave her alone. We don't need friends."

His harsh tone scraped raw wounds to her heart. But what did she expect? Pa had taught her well not to ache for anything from anyone.

He pushed to his feet. "Time to get back to work."

"Right." She hurried to the spot she'd chosen for her house. Too bad he'd already claimed the best site. But never mind. Once she had title to the land she'd use her cabin as an outbuilding and build a real house where she wanted it.

Chapter 3

Trace turned his back to Mandy, ignoring her as she paced out the perimeter of her house and used the butt of her ax to drive in posts.

He harbored a deep desire to kick himself in the behind all around the outside of his house. For a few moments he'd allowed himself to think he was an ordinary man like he'd once been, enjoying friendship with a beautiful woman, listening to her talk, enjoying the sound of her voice. Had he so soon forgotten the lessons he'd learned? As if such were possible with Cora hiding only a few feet away. It knotted his insides to see her go from a buoyant young girl on the cusp of womanhood to this fearful person.

If he had any gumption he'd forget about a race to build a house, march into town, file a claim on the land, then post No Trespassing signs around the whole area.

Except his honor insisted he live up to the agreement they'd given their hands on.

Not for all the gold in the Kootenais would he admit he rather enjoyed the idea of Mandy's company despite her somewhat prickly attitude.

Determined to bring his wayward thoughts into submission, he bent over the log he wanted to place next and set to trimming and notching it. He and Austin had often talked about building their houses. They had promised to help each other. His stomach filled with bile. He never thought his best friend would turn into a lawless Bushwhacker. Thinking about it made his muscles twitch, and he forced his thoughts away from the memory. He could build this house without help.

He might have succeeded in ignoring troublesome Mandy, except she stepped into his peripheral view.

He glanced up to see her studying his place and then hers—which was nothing at this point—with a speculative expression on her face. Only his upbringing stopped him from suggesting she move along and mind her own business. And—a grin tipped one reluctant corner of his mouth—the memory of how quickly she'd taken offense to him saying so a short time ago.

His words and the resulting contest had cost Cora, though Mandy had been nothing but kind and generous— willingly telling Cora all sorts of details about her life.

Letting his ax rest motionless, he considered the woman before him as something she'd said tugged at his mind. He tried to recall what it was. Something about her pa. Then he remembered. "Didn't you say you wanted to go after your pa?"

Her attention jerked toward him, her expression rife with challenge.

He sighed. "Do you walk around looking to be offended, maybe hoping to draw someone into a gunfight?"

Her mouth fell open. She struggled momentarily to close it, and then the burning in her eyes brought him to his feet, ready to defend himself.

"I do not." Her fists clenched and unclenched. "You take that back."

"Nothing to take back. You just proved it." He closed the distance between them until he was just out of reach of her arms. "It might be interesting to know why Mandy Hamilton is so defensive."

She glowered, fit to start his hair on fire. Then she settled back on her heels and gave a mocking smile. "Might be interesting to know why Trace Owens says he doesn't want friends." She correctly read his unspoken denial and grinned in triumph.

"You sure like to get people riled with you."

She lifted one shoulder. "Not normally."

"So it's just me."

"Yup."

He held her gaze as he considered her confession, trying to decide if she wanted to annoy him or... Caution forced him to guard his reaction. "Nice to know you've picked me as your number-one enemy."

"'Twas you who said you didn't want a friend. What else is left?"

He recognized her challenge and decided to ignore it. "There's something about you building a house I don't understand. If you're keen to follow your pa, why would you want something as permanent as a house? Doesn't seem to fit. You sure you're not a wanderer like your pa?"

Denial darkened her eyes, followed swiftly by a flash of confusion as if she'd never considered this conflict between what she said and what she did. Then her lips softened, her eyes glistened.

Mandy looked about to cry.

He couldn't imagine her allowing such weakness.

She blinked away all signs of tears and turned her mouth into a stubborn line. Obviously she would not allow any weeping. "Maybe…" She breathed hard. "Pa might settle down if he had a nice house to live in. You ever think of that?"

He fought between laughing at her question and wanting to somehow assure her that dreams didn't always come true, but a person must go on, making the best of what life handed out.

"Mandy, I…" He had no idea what he meant to say. Only that she brought forth a reaction similar to what he felt when he considered Cora. He chuckled at the idea. Cora, hiding from view in the tent, and Mandy, challenging everything he said, had nothing at all in common. And yet his heart felt the same sort of tightening.

He resisted an urge to pound his closed fist on his forehead.

What was wrong with him today? He returned to shaping the end of the log, pointedly ignoring Mandy while she watched him work. Finally he couldn't stand it another second and glanced up. "Can I help you with something?" He meant the words to be dismissive—a kinder version of *mind your own business*.

"Nope." She didn't move away.

He turned back to his task. Whatever she wanted, she would have to come right out and voice it. He wasn't prepared to play at guessing games.

At last she spun around, grabbed her ax, and stomped into the woods.

Finally. He sat back and drew in a long, refreshing breath.

"Is she gone?" Cora asked after a moment of silence.

"She's taken her ax, so I expect she's off to get logs."

Cora edged back the flap and poked her head out. "You really let her beat you at shooting?"

"I didn't let her. She's a good marksman."

"Don't you mean *markswoman*?"

He turned and caught the flash of mischief in Cora's face. They laughed. "She seemed to want to be friends with you."

Cora shook her head. "I saw her. She's beautiful. She'd be repulsed to see my face. Beautiful people always are."

"I know I'm not beautiful." He pretended a sad note into his voice.

She giggled. "I think you see me the way you want me to be. Maybe the way you remember me."

"I see my little sister. All I have left of my family."

She lowered her head, but not before he caught the glint of tears. Again he vowed to protect her from ignorant people.

"Trace, I'm scared she might lead people here," Cora whispered.

"I've wondered about that, too. Not much I can do about it so long as I don't have title to the land. Except keep a sharp eye out, and discourage any visitors."

Cora snickered. "Like you have with Mandy. She's outshot you and outsmarted you. Wouldn't surprise me none to see her outbuild you, too."

He dropped his ax and pressed his hands to his chest. "Oh such little faith you have in me. I am mortally wounded by your doubt."

She laughed then jerked back inside the tent, pulling the flaps almost closed. She would be able to see out through the tiny opening and watch without anyone being able to see in.

His arms hurt, but it wasn't from work or the heaviness of his ax. It came from regret pulsing from his heart, knowing his little sister would watch life from a protected place, hiding from others. Sweet, funny Cora.

The pain raced both inward and outward until his heart seemed to beat fire and his hands and feet stung as if burned. He should have protected Cora and their parents.

Mandy returned to the clearing, dragging half a dozen spindly trees after her.

"You going to build a log house or a twig shack?" His laughter earned him a look of disdain.

She marched past without answering.

"Hey, Cora, you ought to see this. It reminds me of that fairy tale Mother read. Remember? *The Three Little Pigs*. The middle pig built a house of sticks."

"A house is a house," Mandy muttered. "Don't think we mentioned what we could use to make one." She released her collection of trees and stared at him, hands on hips. "It sounds suspiciously like you've called me a pig."

"Oh brother." He took off his hat and scrubbed his hair. "Here we go again. What's it going to be this time? Swords? Knife throwing?"

She tossed her head, and her thick braid swung over her shoulder. She caught it and returned it to her back.

He followed the movement, suddenly imagining the heavy waterfall of brown waves that would cascade to her waist should she free her hair. He frowned and forced his thoughts back to reality.

"I haven't got time for silly games or silly fairy tales." She gave him a good view of her back and her swinging braid as she bent to lift one of her trees.

He took a step forward, intent on lending aid then stopped and returned to his own building.

"You know," Cora's low voice reached him. "If she's one of the three pigs, that makes you the big bad wolf."

Dare he hope Cora's voice went no further than his ears?

Mandy's roar of laughter dashed his hopes. "Big bad wolf?" She chortled the words. Sucked in air to stop her amusement, made a few wolf-sounding yaps, then dissolved into another fit of laughter.

Cora's muffled giggles wafted from the tent.

Trace tried to be annoyed at her derision, but her full-throated laughter was contagious. He quit resisting and chuckled.

Mandy stopped laughing and dried her eyes. She grinned widely at him.

He couldn't tear himself from her gaze, full of challenge, laughter, and something that dropped into his heart with a warm splash and filled it with sweetness. He hoped she wouldn't see all the things he failed to suppress— hope and despair bonded together like some odd twinning. Surely she would look away, free him from this expectation he couldn't stifle. But she only continued to grin at him.

She quirked one eyebrow. "A wolf? Seems we're pretty familiar with them."

"You never once fooled me with your imitation."

She looked not at all dismayed. "Drew you from the camp though, didn't I?"

"You did a better job at convincing me you were a man."

Faint pink stole up her cheeks. "Didn't take you long to see your mistake, did it?"

His face grew hot, and he wondered if he'd turned as pink as she did.

She jerked away the same instant he turned from her, and he gave every bit of his concentration to preparing each log. In the silence that followed, she grunted and scuffled as she moved her twigs about.

Mandy smiled as she tugged her trees into place. A piggy and a wolf. It was ludicrous. She wondered about this piggy story. Maybe Joanna would know of it.

She should have thought to bring a horse to pull out larger logs, but like Glory said, what did Mandy know about building? She'd studied how Trace constructed the walls on his house. Of course he had newly peeled logs that were much larger than the ones she'd chosen for hers, but the method was surely the same. So she notched her unpeeled logs and laid them out in the square she'd measured out. Big enough for a bed, a table, and small stove but not much more. Live in it. That's all they'd stipulated. But she could see Trace planned a larger, more substantial house. As if he meant to put down roots like an old oak tree and stay forever.

Mandy paused as she tried to imagine a man who stayed because he wanted to. Planned to. So a person could count on him from one day to the next. She understood there were men like that, but her pa had taught her well to question her assumptions.

She placed all her logs and headed back to the woods for more. She hadn't gone far when she realized Trace was also setting out for more logs.

He overtook her as she applied her ax to another tree and stopped to watch, making her too nervous to continue. She straightened and faced him. "You want something?"

"If you notch the tree like this"—he swung his ax to show her what he meant—"the tree will fall that direction. Always check to see what the tree will hit. For instance, you'll want to miss that tree."

"What makes you think so?"

He shrugged. "The branches will get hung up, and you'll have an impossible time getting it down. Besides, look in that crotch. A nest. If I'm not mistaken, it has baby birds in it."

She stared at the spot and tried to reconcile her varying views of this man. A big bad wolf concerned about baby birds and a younger sister. She didn't know what to make of him.

Trace had moved higher up the hill and paused as if something caught his interest. "Mandy, have a look at this view."

It was likely something she'd seen before. In fact, there wasn't a view around here she wasn't familiar with, but she wondered what drew his admiration and climbed to his side.

"You can see up and down the valley for miles. It looks like a good country."

"As good as any, I suppose. There's plenty of game, not too many people, and if I believed all the tales, rubies and gold and other treasures ready for the picking."

"Sounds like you don't believe it."

"Just 'cause someone says it, don't make it true."

He pulled his gaze from the view to study her.

She met his look, letting him know she would defend her statement if need be.

"You're one suspicious woman, you know that? Don't you trust anyone?"

"Only God and my sisters." Though sometimes she found it easier to trust her sisters. At least she could demand an explanation from Glory or Joanna. Seems with God you just had to accept what He sent your way, even if you didn't understand the whys or wherefores. Levi said that's what faith was.

Trace continued to study her. "Guess we're in much the same situation. I only trust my sister, and I try to trust God." He looked regretful. "Sometimes it's not easy to do."

Their gazes went on and on, silently sharing secret doubts and fears, and so much more she couldn't begin to understand. "So what's your reason?" she asked.

"For what?"

"Being so narrow in your trust." She almost shivered at how quickly his expression changed before he turned back to eyeing the view.

"I guess everyone has their grounds."

"True." But not everyone's reasons made a sister hide inside a tent during the heat of the day nor turn a man's expression to granite in the blink of an eye.

"I see someone riding up the other side." He pointed. "Riding like a madman."

She moved closer. Saw the rider. "It's Glory. She always rides crazy. She's going to see her preacher man."

Trace chuckled. "You say that with a great deal of expression, but I can't tell if it's pride or regret or something else."

She tipped her head to consider it. "I suppose it's both. Glory is too wild to marry a preacher, but Levi doesn't seem to mind."

"So what's the regret?"

She thought she'd spoken both, but his question forced the truth to the surface. "Our family is getting divided into pieces. I'm not sure I like it."

"It's part of life. I thought all girls looked forward to growing up and getting married. I know Cora did."

The way his voice dropped and he clamped his mouth shut, Mandy knew he meant she had at one time, but that time was over. She wondered why. Tried to think of a way to frame a question. But he spoke again before she could.

"Now we have a new home to look forward to and a new life. At least if I don't spend my days staring out at the view." He clucked at the horse and moved on.

Mandy stayed where she was, watching Glory until she raced out of sight. Good thing Joanna couldn't see her reckless haste or she'd worry. With a deep sigh, she turned away.

Trace had chosen a tree not far away and tackled it with the ax. A wide stance allowed him a generous swing at the trunk. She watched the muscles across his back work with each swing. A strong man. A gentle man who considered the safety of tiny birds. But a man with a secret that made him deny friendship and keep his sister in hiding.

The sort of man she would do well to steer clear of.

And yet…

She pushed her hat more firmly on her head. What did it matter? She'd build her house, sleep in it, and win the land. He'd have to move somewhere else. He and his secretive sister.

Mindful of the lesson on falling trees, she cut down more spindly things and dragged them back. By the time Trace returned, she had several more in place. He might bring in bigger ones, but she could set six for every one of his, so it equaled out.

She stared at the position of the sun. Time to return to the stopping house and help Joanna. Which left Trace plenty of time to continue building without competition. "I have to go help my sister."

He nodded. "Fine by me."

"Well, it's not fine by me. It's not fair. You can work several hours more a day than I can."

He spared her the briefest of glances. "Don't remember anything in our agreement about having to work the same hours."

"A gentleman would offer."

He didn't even bother to lift his head but continued trimming the log. "A lady would honor her word."

"Surely you don't expect me to neglect my duties at home? That wouldn't be fair to Joanna." She loaded every word with as much guilt as she could dredge up, hoping to persuade him to agree he wouldn't work when she wasn't able to.

"Mandy Hamilton, I can't believe you're trying to change the rules after we've agreed. You could have specified any conditions before the fact. But not after."

"Oh." She clenched her hands into fists. "I perceive you are a most unreasonable man."

That brought him to his feet to stride toward her. He didn't stop until they were toe-to-toe. She met his glare with one equally as narrow-eyed.

"I do not consider it unreasonable to expect a person—man or woman—to honor an agreement. To live up to what they've promised. Or to be loyal to another."

She stared, surprised at his words, then backed up a pace. "I will indeed honor our agreement if you are unwilling to concede to changes. As to promises and loyalty, I think you are not talking about me."

He pulled himself taller and crossed his arms over his chest. "I expect nothing less than complete trustworthiness."

Again she wondered if he meant her. But how could he? He had no more reason to trust her than she had to count on him.

She didn't trust easily. Certainly wouldn't be opening her heart to a man full of dark secrets. A man who said promises had no value, loyalty was to be questioned, stated he didn't need friendship…and was hiding his sister.

He turned back to his task. Clearly he could not be trusted.

She would not let little hints of kindness and brotherly loyalty cause her to think otherwise.

Chapter 4

The evening chores done and the guests settled down for the night, the three sisters withdrew to their bedroom.

Joanna opened up their mother's Bible. Shortly after Levi had shown up in Bonners Ferry, they'd begun the habit of reading from the scriptures. Joanna sat on her bed facing Glory and Mandy, who shared a bed—at least, until the wedding in a few more weeks.

Mandy tried not to think of one of her sisters moving on. The bed would seem wide and lonely without Glory. Glory was a year old when Mandy was born. She couldn't remember a time she wasn't able to reach out and touch the comforting presence of her sister. Or turn to their eldest sister for comfort and guidance.

Joanna studied each of them as she spoke. "Levi read from the Psalms on Sunday. I enjoyed it so much I thought I'd read there tonight." She turned a few pages. "Psalm one hundred forty-six." And she read.

Mandy listened, hoping for an answer for the turmoil in her heart. She didn't want Trace on her land. She didn't want to be his friend, even though she offered to befriend Cora. And why did Cora hide? Most of all, why did Mandy's thoughts head one direction then switch to something else whenever she was around him? In fact, he was nowhere near, and it was happening again.

"'Put not your trust in princes, nor in the son of man, in whom there is no help.'"

Mandy pressed her fingers to her mouth to stifle a giggle.

Joanna stopped reading. "What's funny?"

"God telling us not to trust men." Her chuckle was half snort.

Glory pushed her, causing her to fall over on the pillow. "Not all men are untrustworthy... ."

Joanna and Mandy knew what was coming next. They chorused the words with her. "Levi's not."

The three of them grinned at each other.

Mandy righted herself. "Glory, I wish you weren't leaving."

"We can't stay like this forever."

Ignoring them, Joanna finished reading the Psalm and closed the Bible. "Mandy, what's this about a man up in the hills?"

Glory nudged Mandy, signaling she'd told Joanna.

Mandy jabbed her elbow in Glory's ribs, thanking her for interfering. "All kinds of men in the hills."

"And building a house? What's that all about?"

Mandy gave Joanna her best innocent, wide-eyed expression. Not that she expected Joanna to be fooled. For half a penny, Mandy would love to tell her to mind her own business. Remind her she wasn't Mandy's mother.

But she knew it would hurt her sister's feelings, so she held back the words.

Glory decided she had the right to answer for Mandy. "You know how Mandy always picks out a spot for a house. She can't stop thinking Pa will come back, and we'll be a family." She turned to Mandy. "I keep telling you to give up on Pa. He ain't got time for us, and besides, it's too late. We're grown up. Ready to start our own homes."

Mandy tightened her jaw. Knew she looked stubborn and petulant but didn't care. "I'd welcome Pa back if he came."

Glory grabbed Mandy's shoulder and shook her a little. "Think. When has Pa ever come looking for us? Never. We follow him. Or we used to. But no more. Stop pinning your hopes on him."

Joanna's soft voice interrupted. "About this man…"

"He's on my land." She ignored the way Joanna's eyebrows went up. Glory snorted.

"I tried to chase him off but he wouldn't go. So we agreed that whoever builds a house first can file for the deed."

Joanna leaned forward. "Exactly how did you try and get rid of him?"

At the same time Glory groaned. "You don't know how to build a house."

Mandy chose to hear only Glory's words and waved her hand dismissively. "We didn't stipulate what sort of a house it had to be. Only that we had to live in it."

"Let me guess." Glory sounded resigned. "You're not building a regular house."

"Well. I'll be able to live in it. That's all that matters." She described the rough structure she intended to put up. "Trace is putting up a real log house." She told of his work.

"Trace is the man?" Joanna prompted.

"Trace Owens. And he has a sister who hides." That brought a burst of interest from both sisters. "I've had only two glimpses of her. One from the hillside. And one when I won a shooting match with him." Another flurry of interest and more explanation.

When she finished telling how she'd outshot the man, Joanna and Glory laughed.

Mandy waited for their amusement to abate. "Joanna, did you ever hear a story of the three pigs and a big bad wolf?"

"Yes, I read it when I worked for the Johnsons. Mrs. Johnson bought a new storybook for Sally. That was one of the stories."

"Tell me what it was about."

Joanna told of three pigs who built houses—one of straw, one of sticks, and one of bricks. A big bad wolf blew down the first two houses, hoping to eat the pigs, but they found shelter in the brick house and captured the big bad wolf in a pot of boiling water.

Mandy grinned. She liked what happened to the wolf. It meant she won.

Her sisters demanded an explanation.

But she would never admit he'd likened her to the middle pig. "He's so confident he'll beat me. But I can out do him without even trying." She snorted. "The arrogant man." Joanna and Glory chuckled and exchanged knowing looks.

"What?"

"Nothing—except he sounds like the perfect man for you." Glory had the nerve to speak the words, but Joanna nodded.

"He is not." Mandy bounded off the bed and faced her sisters with clenched fists.

Glory nodded, too. "Yup. He is. He shoots almost as well as you. Enough to earn a bit of admiration. And he's building a solid house. What you've always wanted."

"You. Are. So. Wrong. This man has all kinds of secrets. Why his sister refuses to leave the tent. I don't trust him. The last thing I need is a man I have to guess about."

Joanna gave her serious study. "I wonder if you'll ever let yourself trust a man no matter how noble and true he is."

"'Course I will." But he'd have to prove himself able to live up to her expectations. "I'm going to bed." She stripped off her trousers and shirt and pulled on an oversize man's nightshirt.

Glory shook her head sadly. "Better start wearing something a little more feminine than that if you ever expect a man to look at you."

Mandy's face burned like fury. She grabbed a pillow and whacked Glory on the head. "No man better see me like this unless he's married to me."

Glory fell down on the bed, giggling madly. "You'll want to look all pretty and nice for the man you marry. You wait and see."

Mandy whacked her again for good measure. "You still wear trousers. Besides how many fancy nightgowns have you made?"

Glory grabbed the pillow and tucked it under her head. "I might make a couple. You never know."

Joanna turned off the lamp. "Girls, go to sleep."

Mandy and Glory giggled just like they always did when Joanna grew motherly.

But Mandy couldn't fall asleep as a thousand questions raced through her mind. What did Cora hide? Why was

Trace so touchy about friends and loyalty? Was he really intent on staying or just unable to resist a challenge? Where did he come from and why?

And what made her heart float high up her throat just thinking of him?

The next morning, she hurried about her chores, chomping with impatience, knowing Trace would spend these hours raising the walls of his house higher and higher.

But finally she could leave. As usual, she called, "Be back later."

Joanna came to the door. "Hunting for meat or for men?" She laughed.

Mandy flicked her the barest protesting glare then hurried up the trail. She wasn't hunting any man.

In fact, she was doing her best to drive him away.

Trace had been up since before dawn. After Mandy left yesterday he'd raised the walls by four logs, but he had a long way to go and planned to use every hour to his advantage.

"Breakfast is ready." Cora sat by the campfire, her bonnet hiding her face.

"I don't have time to eat."

"You must eat. You can't keep working so hard while starving yourself." She paused. "I wish you'd let me help."

She'd offered several times but Trace's imagination pictured her being crushed by a runaway log. He would never let anything harm his little sister again.

"It would go faster with two of us working. We'd be sure to win the contest and get the land. Otherwise…" She left the rest unsaid.

"I have no intention of losing this place and my house to Mandy." He turned to study Mandy's structure.

Cora joined him. "It isn't much of a house."

"Like she said, we didn't specify the sort of house it should be."

"Maybe you should do something similar. Just to win the land."

He contemplated the idea for several moments, shifting his gaze between the two houses. "No. I think I can win and still build a solid structure. Something we can live in for a long time."

"Do you suppose we will be happy here?"

"As happy as we dare."

"Life will never be the same." She hunched forward, clutching her bonnet closer. "Do you think the Bushwhackers will follow us?"

"They got what they wanted. They got rid of the Owenses. I don't expect we'll hear from them again."

"Then why do you always keep the rifle so close and jerk up from bed at the slightest sound?"

He would not admit his fear that one of the marauding bunch would take it upon himself to track down Trace and Cora and finish what they'd started. "There could be wild animals around."

"Like Mandy pretending to be a wolf?" She giggled.

"Glad you find it amusing."

"Admit it. She's funny. I can never guess what she might say or do next."

"About as funny as a case of cholera."

Cora laughed.

Trace tried to recall the last time she'd shown so much pure, sweet enjoyment. He allowed himself a brief moment of appreciation for Mandy if her presence allowed Cora to laugh.

"She doesn't put up with any nonsense from you."

Trace faced his sister. "Are you saying I'm overbearing? Difficult to get along with?"

Cora backed up a space and held her hands up in mock defensiveness. "Heaven forbid. But…" She slowed her words. "Since the fire, you have grown…well, hard."

"Guess I've been forced to get that way."

"I know. And I'm not condemning you. But when Mandy is here, you seem to forget about the past. For just a bit."

"Maybe because she forces me to be on my toes. She continually surprises me." He shook his head. "Who'd ever think she might put up a twig house?"

"Like the second little piggy. Don't think she fancied being called a piggy."

"Don't imagine she would. But at least she didn't challenge me to a gunfight at high noon."

They both laughed. It felt good and cleansing.

"Let's eat breakfast." Cora took his arm and guided him to the fire to dish out thick oatmeal mush and fresh biscuits cooked in the outdoor oven. "I put stew to simmer. It will do us for lunch. You'll have to bring me some if Mandy is here."

"Cora, I don't like you being holed up in the heat of the day."

"I'm fine. I stay close to the flap. I get air there."

Meaning she didn't intend to venture forth and allow anyone to see her.

"I'd sooner take the heat than have people make faces or call me names."

They'd ridden through one town during daylight hours, and a woman had screamed and called Cora a witch. They would have been run out of town except they left as fast as they could.

He pulled her close. "People like that don't matter."

Except they both knew they did. "Just as soon as I finish this house you'll have a nice place to stay. I'll put in windows to let in air."

"I'll put up curtains to prevent prying eyes."

He hurried through breakfast and returned to the house. Not only did he need to beat Mandy, the sooner he completed it, the sooner Cora could get out of the inadequate tent and have decent shelter.

Somewhere to his right, a wolf yapped. "Mandy's coming," he warned. Cora ducked into the tent.

She didn't show up right away, but the sound of an ax and the crack of trees falling echoed through the woods. She was working on her stick house, but he intended to beat her. He bent his back to preparing and placing the logs he'd dragged in late last evening.

Mandy grunted as she dragged in her twigs.

"Why don't you use a horse?"

She dropped her load and shrugged. "Prefer to prove I can win by my own efforts." She dusted her hands and strode toward him. With a measuring glance she studied how much he'd done since she left. "Thought you'd have it up to here by now." She indicated her shoulder. "Been slacking off, have you?"

"Didn't want to get too far ahead of you. Didn't seem gentlemanly, and it seems I have to prove I'm that."

She grinned as if she knew something vastly amusing at his expense then bent to examine the notching of his logs. "You did a fine job. A fine job. Can't say as I mind seeing the house built soundly." She faced him, her eyes flashing challenge.

Good thing he had stopped using the ax. He might have cut his hand, because his heart stuttered at the way her eyes blazed, filling him with a strange sensation. Like he'd been riding along mindlessly and his horse had dropped over a sharp edge, taking him along for the descent and leaving his heart to follow.

She didn't blink. "You realize the house will be mine when I win this little challenge?"

"Not when. Not if. When I win, your little pile of twigs will be nothing more than a corn crib or"—he tried to think of some use of significant unimportance—"pigpen."

"Speaking of pigs…"

Why did she continue to grin so triumphantly? And why did he feel as if he'd been invited along for an adventure?

No way. He would guard against any invitation from any source from now on.

She continued. "You do know what happened to the big bad wolf in your story of the three pigs, don't you?"

"He had pork dinner. Yum. Yum." Only he knew it hadn't ended well for the wolf, and he wondered if he should heed the warning.

"Nope. The pigs outsmarted him. Sometimes it isn't the biggest or the baddest who win."

"I'll take that under consideration." Too bad he couldn't believe it. Seems the biggest and the worst did win. And the small and decent lost…. Paid with everything they had. He straightened.

"I've only got a few hours to work, so no time for idle conversation."

But did she walk away and tend to her own affairs? No, she stood staring at the walls of his house.

"Seems to me it's going to be a lot of work for one man to get the logs up to roof level. Hmm. Let's see how the big bad wolf handles that." And she marched away.

He knew she wasn't wishing him well. "Takes longer for one man, but by applying some basic mechanical know-how, it can be done." More time, more physical effort, but he could and would do it.

"If you say so." She chanted a tuneless ditty as she worked.

After a moment, he made out the words.

"I'm not afraid of the big bad wolf."

"Psst." Cora called for his attention.

He left his work to see what she needed.

"Why is she so confident?"

He wondered the same thing. "It's all bluff."

"I don't know. I don't trust her."

"I'll keep an eye on her." Neither of them said they weren't ready to trust anyone.

He returned to his work, doing his best to ignore the endless cycle of words coming from Mandy as she worked. "I'm not afraid of the big bad wolf." He could almost believe she repeated the singsong dirge without thought…but not quite. It was part of her strategy. And he didn't like it one bit.

He pried the next log into place, struggling to raise it to the next level. Sweat poured from him as he worked.

The endless tune from Mandy came to an end but only because she watched him lifting the heavy log. It would have made a world of difference to have someone hold one end steady while he hoisted the other, but he wouldn't ask her for help if his life depended on it and was equally certain she'd refuse if he did.

The log slid into place, and Mandy clapped.

Not about to let anything she did annoy him—or rather let her know it did—he bowed deeply then headed for the water bucket. He downed two dipperfuls, took off his hat, and poured another dipperful over his head.

Mandy stared as he shook the water from his hair then spun away as if he'd splashed her. He knew he hadn't.

But she didn't return to her own house. Instead she sidled up to Trace. "It must be awfully hot in that tent. Why don't you let Cora come out?"

"Let her?" He sputtered. "You think I'm forcing her to stay there?"

"Nothing else makes sense. It must be hot as an oven. If you let her sit in the shade she'd be so much cooler." There was no gentle pleading in her voice, only hard, accusing tones that stung Trace clear to the tips of his ears.

"I am not making her stay. She doesn't want to come out." He shot out each word with fury. How dare she accuse him of such unkindness?

"Prove it. Tell her she can come out."

"Mandy Hamilton, there are some things you should stay out of, and this is one."

She jammed her fists on her hips. "So you can't prove it."

"I don't need to prove anything to you. Best you just leave this alone."

"So you've said, but I take orders from no one."

"Kind of figured that was your problem."

"Don't consider it a problem."

"Think what you want, but Cora won't come out even if I beg."

"Prove it."

He took a step toward her. "If you were a man—"

"Don't let that stop you." She widened her stance and held her hands in front as if she truly expected him to engage in another wrestling match with her.

He turned his back to her, thought better of it considering some of her little habits like kicking and biting and goodness knows what else, and faced her again. "You are the most infuriating woman I have ever met."

"And you are the most devious man I've ever met, and

that's going some. I've met a lot of male creatures, especially in the stopping house, and I gotta say some are pretty nasty people."

He'd only once before seen a red haze in his vision. And it had taken a whole lot more than one woman to cause that. "Cora, come out and prove to this…this…" He refused to say *woman*. "…person that you are not some sort of prisoner."

Cora gasped. Next followed a silence so deep he could hear the beat of his own heart and the flap of wings on a bird passing overhead.

"She's accusing me of forcing you to stay in the tent."

"I don't want to come out. I won't." Cora's voice trembled. "Mandy, Miss Hamilton, believe me, it's not because of Trace. It's my own choice. Please, just leave me alone."

"There." Trace had never glared at a woman before like he glared at Mandy. "Are you satisfied?"

She didn't look one bit convinced. "There's something mighty fishy around here, and it ain't fish." But she strode over, picked up her ax, and headed for the woods.

He waited until she crashed out of sight. Allowed himself a small smile. Not like her to be so noisy. She must really be annoyed. But she had no reason. Any more than she had any need of the truth.

He brought his attention back to his sister. Cora would be in fear and trembling until she knew she was safe. "She's gone."

"Why is she so set on seeing me?"

"I can't say. Maybe she's truly concerned about you staying in the tent in this heat." Or maybe she thought she had a right to know everyone's business. Or maybe she suspected them of some deep, dark secret, though he couldn't imagine what two travelers—a brother and sister with nothing more than what they could carry with them in way of belongings—could be suspected of concealing.

Except Cora was hiding, and that piqued Mandy's curiosity.

He didn't trust her to let it go, but he didn't know what to expect next.

What an unsettling woman.

Chapter 5

Mandy worked like a fiend putting up log after log. Never mind that Trace called them twigs. They were making walls, and that's all she cared about.

She tried to ignore him as he worked, steadily building the walls higher on his house. It was a fine-looking building. She'd be right proud to be its owner in a short while. She tried hard not to think about his sister, Cora, while the sun beat down. Even out in the open with a breeze against Mandy's hot skin, the heat was close to unbearable.

"Aren't you afraid she'll perish from the heat?" she demanded as she paused to down some tepid water from her canteen. She thought longingly of the cold water in the river not far away. But she wouldn't waste time to fetch it.

"She's fine."

"How do you know? Did you check to see? How can you ignore her?"

He flung around. "Seems you worry about her enough for the two of us." But he stomped over to the tent and ducked inside.

She listened shamelessly.

"Mandy is sure you're going to die in here. Are you?" As he spoke the anger in his voice fled and his words gentled. "It is dreadfully hot. Cora, let me take you to the shade."

"No. I'm fine."

"Cora, you'll be just as fine outside."

"No I won't."

Mandy held her breath and leaned close to catch Cora's whisper.

"She'll see me."

"I'll hide you by those bushes up the hill a ways. No one will see you."

"No. Just leave me. I'm fine."

"Fine." The word sounded angry.

Mandy stepped away and bent over one of her logs.

"She's fine." Trace's tone did not indicate any relief, but he, too, returned to shaping logs.

Even at lunchtime, Cora refused to leave the tent.

Mandy grew more and more curious. She'd seen glimpses of Cora and could think of no reason the girl would be afraid for others to see her.

Something was not right here.

And Mandy intended to find out what it was.

The afternoon sun, unrelenting in its heat, headed for the west. Time for Mandy to return to her chores back in Bonners Ferry. She stood back to study the progress on her house.

"One good wind and it will blow away." Trace sounded downright happy about the idea.

"Wouldn't gloat just yet. Unless…" She spun about

to eye him with suspicion. "Seems in the story the wolf had something to do with the fall of the first two houses. Don't you be planning to do something to my house."

He let out a *tsk*. "You are one mistrustful woman. Fact is, it never crossed my mind." He tipped his head one way and then the other as he studied her house. "Looks a little askew to me."

"It's a good enough house for me. I guarantee it won't disintegrate in the wind or the snow. What it lacks in beauty it makes up for in strength."

He had the gall to laugh openly.

"A gentleman would show more respect."

"Ah, but you forget, I'm really the big bad wolf." He puffed out his cheeks and blew at her house then faced her, his gaze filled with teasing.

She gasped. Not because he pretended to blow her house down but because like sunlight on water, his eyes flashed with blue brightness, allowing her to see something she'd not noticed before.

The man was as handsome as any man she'd ever seen. And when he smiled like that, he seemed to make the world a happy place.

She forced her unwilling attention to something beyond his left shoulder. Tried to think what she was supposed to be doing. Her gaze settled on the ax. Then the walls of her house. Drifted onward to the hill beyond, where the trees glistened with heat and birds twittered softly. A chickadee flitted between branches seeking food for her nestlings.

Food. Mandy's thoughts slowly righted themselves. "Time for me to go. The stopping house is in need of fresh meat." She brought her gaze back to Trace, relieved to see he had returned to his usual guarded look. "See you tomorrow. Bye, Cora," she called.

"Bye." Surprise filled the single word coming from the tent.

Mandy strode off, grinning, though for the life of her she couldn't explain why.

A little later she took game to Joanna then slipped noiselessly back up the narrow trail toward Trace and Cora's camp. She circled to a hill overlooking the site where she knew Trace wouldn't bother her. The trees there were too small for him to want to chop down. The brush allowed her to edge close to the clearing for a good view.

She found a spot allowing her to see the front of the tent and settled back to watch.

Trace worked on a log. Did the man ever leave off building the house?

Mandy measured his progress, checked it against what she'd accomplished earlier, and nodded. She still held her own.

There was no sign of Cora. Surely she didn't remain in the tent after Mandy left. But Trace seemed to be talking to someone.

Mandy edged to her left until she could see around the log wall. Cora was there all right, sitting with her back to the wall, plucking blades of grass and examining them. Her mouth moved as she talked to Trace, but Mandy was too far away to hear her, and she'd never learned to read lips. Too bad. It would have come in handy at the moment.

Trace dragged the log to the wall, rolled it into place. He dusted his hands as he stood back and admired his work, obviously well pleased with his efforts.

Huh. It was way too soon for him to think he could gloat.

He took his horse and headed back up the hill for another log. Good. Now she could watch Cora without the distraction of Trace.

She edged closer until she couldn't go any farther without fear of discovery. Cora still sat against the log wall, her bonnet practically covering her face.

In the distance, the ringing of an ax informed her of Trace's whereabouts. The thump of a falling tree soon followed. He would be busy trimming and barking it for some time.

Mandy simply had to wait and watch Cora.

Cora stretched her arms skyward as if embracing the world or imploring God to change it. Mandy couldn't say which. A breeze fluttered the leaves. Cora shoved her bonnet to her shoulders and shook her head as if inviting a breath of coolness. She bent to get a pot off the ground and take it to the fire where she hung it to cook the contents.

That's when Mandy saw her face. One cheek beautiful as china. The other red and puckered.

"Oh no." She mouthed the words. *So this is what she didn't want people to see.*

"I guessed you wouldn't let it go."

She jumped to her feet like a frightened deer and jerked around to stare at Trace. "Where did you come from?"

"You're not the only one who can tiptoe through the trees." His narrowed eyes warned he wasn't pleased to see her.

She saw his anger and something more. Something that made her want to reach out and touch him, assure him things weren't as bad as he and Cora seemed to think. But tension vibrated through him, and she knew any sudden movement on her part would bring forth some sort of eruption. Instead she leaned back, hoping her attempt to appear relaxed would neutralize his tautness.

"Now you know why she doesn't want anyone to see her."

She nodded. "What happened?"

"She was burned."

"How dreadful for her."

"She will never forget it. And if she tried, neither her mirror nor other people's stares would let her."

"I didn't mean her scar. I meant being burned. It must have been painful."

"More than you can imagine." His eyes lost their anger and flooded with despair. "She deserves to be left alone."

"Deserves? Or do you mean desires? But she's a beautiful young woman. I can't imagine she wants to spend the rest of her life hiding."

"What she wants and what she has to deal with are entirely different things."

Mandy sat on the ground, cushioned with old leaves and pine needles, and turned to watch Cora.

"Can't you show a little decency and leave us in peace?"

"I'm not bothering anyone. Just sitting here enjoying the afternoon shade." She wanted to say something more, but she didn't even know what it was. She needed time to clarify her thoughts and put them into words. "You're welcome to join me." She patted the ground beside her.

He grunted. Or was it a groan? "What have I done that deserves this kind of torture?"

"Are you referring to the heat? Or the flies? Maybe the work of building a house?" She knew he meant none of those things, but she would not give him the satisfaction of acknowledging what he meant.

"I mean you. From the first day you have tormented me."

She grinned up at him. "You're just sore because I upset your plans."

"I couldn't have said it better." But the anger and despair fled. He glanced at the spot she'd indicated beside her and shrugged as if to say he didn't have much choice because he expected she wouldn't leave him any peace until he sat. With a great show of reluctance he joined her. "I don't suppose it would do any good to suggest you forget you've seen her."

"Why would I want to forget it?"

"She doesn't want people to know."

She understood he meant know about her disfiguring scars, but she wouldn't accept it. "I am not repulsed by her face, if that's what you expect."

He didn't say anything, which she found oddly touching. But when she turned to study him, his face was a mask of disbelief.

"Her face is scarred horribly."

"Only part of one cheek, not her whole face. And it's only a tiny fraction of her physical body and nothing to do with who she is."

"Huh."

"I've seen people who are whole and even beautiful, but their spirits are scarred terribly by greed or bitterness or cruelty. I've seen people who are ugly and deformed but have such an inner beauty you never think about how they look." The words she'd been trying to sort out tumbled forth in a tangled rush. "Where we once lived there was a bent little man who had a hump in his back and one side of his face twisted all out of sorts, but Old Terry was the sweetest person I've ever known." Her voice tightened, revealing how fond she had been of the old man. "He understood how three girls forced to live with an unwelcome family could feel abandoned and unloved. So every day as we walked to school, Old Terry would meet us. He'd walk a little ways with us. We had to slow down for him to keep up, and he only went a short distance before he was out of breath. But every day he gave us something. Maybe only a pretty rock to put in our pockets."

She sniffed, hoping he wouldn't notice as unshed tears clogged her nose. It had been a long time since she'd thought of Old Terry, and she wondered how she could have forgotten him and the lessons he'd taught them—like finding happiness and joy in little things, accepting the bad without letting it destroy them. If only she could make Trace and Cora see life like Old Terry had. "Sometimes he found a wildflower, or a bit of pretty glass. Many times it was only a kind word, a reminder of better things."

She'd been lounging over her knees but suddenly sat up straight and blinked back her threatening tears. "I just remembered. One thing Old Terry would bring us was Bible verses written on a scrap of paper. I used to keep them in a little cigar box." She turned to look at Trace. "I can't believe I forgot that." A sudden rush of memories washed over her. "He said we should always trust God no matter what happened, believe God had nothing but good planned for us."

Trace watched her closely, a flicker of amusement in his eyes. But she saw something more and recognized it as the same mixture of despair and hope Old Terry had noticed in her and her sisters.

"I remember the verse he gave us one day and made us promise to memorize. For days afterward he would make us repeat it until we could say it easily."

"What verse was that?" Trace's voice sounded as thick

as hers had felt a few seconds ago. "Do you still remember it?"

"As if I could forget. Jeremiah twenty-nine, verse eleven. 'For I know the thoughts that I think toward you, saith the Lord, thoughts of peace, and not of evil, to give you an expected end.' He said it meant God had nothing but good for us in His thoughts."

Trace's gaze held her firm. Searching, hoping, delving into her heart as if seeking some balm there.

She let him look his fill, prayed God would comfort and encourage him with the verse as it had her when Old Terry gave it to her.

He blinked and shook his head. "Hard to believe God has anything good in mind in what happened to Cora."

"Let me meet her. Really meet her."

"I can't do that. I promised to protect her."

"By hiding her?"

He closed his eyes as if to shut out her demands.

"She shouldn't hide from people. What a lonely life. I would think it might be a worse fate than being burned."

"Mandy." He groaned. "You don't know what you're talking about."

"Yes, I do. For instance, if Old Terry had hidden just because some people were unkind… Some threw rocks at him and called him a devil. But if he'd let them turn him into a recluse, who would have helped and encouraged three lonely girls?" She touched Trace's arm in an appeal to give her words consideration. "Let me meet her."

He covered her hand with his, a warm sense of connection flowing through her arm to her heart. She wanted to help him, ease his pain, help Cora.

"You almost persuade me, but it's not my decision."

"You know, I can steal in silently and meet her if you don't warn her of my approach."

"And be a traitor to my own sister?" He shook her hand off and scrambled to his feet. "If she can't trust her own brother, who can she trust?"

"She can trust me. You can, too."

He bent close. "Can I trust you to respect Cora's desire to be left alone?"

She rose to her feet to face him squarely. "I will not agree to something I am so opposed to."

"Then don't ask me to trust you." He stomped into the woods and disappeared.

She stood still for a moment then nodded, having come to a firm decision.

She would not take no for an answer.

He heard her following him. Obviously, she meant him to or she wouldn't have made so much noise. He returned to where he'd left the horse, but he wouldn't go back to the camp with Mandy trailing after him like a lost dog. He faced her. "Why are you following me?" The stubborn set of her jaw made him want to grind his teeth. With two steps he closed the distance between them and grabbed her shoulders to shake her. "Mandy, leave us alone."

Awareness hit him on several levels. Her shoulders were firm. Muscles twitched beneath his palms. She was a strong woman, and he meant both physically and morally. He stopped shaking her but did not pull his hands away.

She pressed her hands to his shoulders in a manner imitating the way he'd captured her, and he wondered if she felt aggravation as well or something else. Her expression hinted at patience and understanding.

"Trace, if I came across an injured animal in the woods, I would not walk away until I'd done all I could to help it." Her smile flashed with unspoken promises. "Why would I do any less for a hurting person?"

He forced words from his thick brain. "Because people have the ability to say whether or not they want help."

She nodded, holding his gaze in an unrelenting grasp.

He couldn't break away even if he tried. But he discovered he didn't want to. Something in her look offered him hope, healing, or… He couldn't say what. He didn't try to make sense of his mixed-up thoughts.

She patted one shoulder. "You know I won't let this go, so you might as well accept it."

He shifted his gaze, freeing himself from her power. "It isn't just about you and me. It's Cora and her wishes."

"You know it's wrong to keep her like this." She tilted her head toward the camp.

He'd thought it himself a time or two. But… "You haven't seen the way people react to her."

She shrugged her shoulders, sending a thousand sparks into his palms.

He dropped his hands and spun away. What was he to do? Not that she was giving him any choice. She would follow him, dog him, harass him, spout forth insults until she got her way. Might as well get it over with.

Ignoring her, neither giving her permission to follow him or ordering her not to, he led the horse back to camp.

Of course, she followed as he knew she would.

They broke into the clearing. Cora glanced up. Her gaze went past Trace, and she bolted to her feet.

"I couldn't get rid of her," Trace said, regret and sadness making a twisted rope of his insides.

Cora clutched at her neck, looking for her bonnet, but it had fallen to the ground. Gasping, pressing her hand to her cheek, she started toward the tent and ground to a halt when she saw Mandy blocking her path.

"Don't be afraid," Mandy soothed.

Cora whimpered. "Go away." She ducked, giving Mandy a view of the top of her head.

"I don't aim to hurt you."

Trace watched. Part of him wanted to bodily remove Mandy from the face of the earth—or at least return her to Bonners Ferry and nail her to the floor of the stopping house. Another part wanted to see how this played out. Could she persuade Cora not to hide?

Mandy caught Cora's chin and tipped her face up. She stroked one cheek and then the other. "You are much too young and beautiful to hide."

Cora's blue eyes widened. She looked hopeful, as if she wanted to believe Mandy.

Trace could not get in a satisfying breath. His little sister had been born with a halo of golden-white hair. It had darkened slightly as she grew. In the fire she'd lost much of her hair on one side but no one would know it to look at her now. It had grown back enough for Cora to braid it into tidy submission.

But despite her beautiful eyes and hair, Cora would never be the same. He recalled something Mandy had said. Cora was scarred both inside and out.

Trace admitted he was equally scarred inside. Nothing could change that.

With a muffled sound—half groan, half cry—Cora broke free of Mandy and scrambled to find her bonnet and tie it tight. She glanced at the tent, stole a fleeting look at Mandy, then turned her back to them and walked to the half-built log house. She slipped around the corner and sank to the ground, holding the edge of her bonnet to her cheek.

Mandy shifted her attention to Trace, her eyes brimming with sorrow and sympathy. She smiled. Did he detect a quiver in her lips?

"It's a start," she murmured.

Why did her words fill him with hope such as he'd forgotten existed? It pushed at the bottom of his heart, sought to escape into his thoughts, his feelings, his life. He tried to shake himself free of her gaze and failed.

He dare not allow himself such a measure of hope.

He could not, would not let himself trust her. "Time to get to work," he muttered. He dragged the log to the house, unhitched the horse, and set it free to graze. All the while Mandy remained, watching. And no doubt scheming something.

He could hardly wait to see what it was. Mocking, silent laughter caught halfway up his throat. So far her schemes had brought him nothing but trouble.

So why then did he grin?

Chapter 6

Mandy tried to make sense of what happened up the hill. Why had he touched her? Why had she grabbed his shoulders in a similar gesture? The way her insides bucked at his touch should have warned her. But did she listen to the signals? No. She was far too intent on convincing him it was wrong to let Cora hide. But when she'd felt his warm flesh under her palms, recognized the strength there, acknowledged the twitch of his muscles, and experienced a helpless tangle of thoughts and emotions, she realized she had stepped into something she was at a loss to control.

Even now, after focusing her attention on Cora, her insides contained a whirlwind of confusion. Cora. She pushed her thoughts, her attention back to the girl who again wore her bonnet like a helmet of steel. At least she hadn't retreated to the heat of the tent.

Mandy nodded decisively. She knew what to do next. Hang about for a time to prove to Cora she posed no harm.

Trace sat astride the log, about two feet from where Cora hunkered against the wall. Neither spoke, though the air was heavy with silent words.

Mandy grabbed her ax and plunked down on the other end of the log, imitating Trace's movements as he stripped bark from the tree.

He stopped work.

She felt his demanding look. "What? You've never seen a woman debark a tree?"

"I never thought to see Mandy Hamilton assisting Trace Owens."

She shrugged and returned to her task. "Consider yourself fortunate indeed, because you won't see it very long."

"Why am I seeing it at all?"

"You looked like you needed help." She slid him a teasing glance. "No need to let a little competition stop us from being neighborly."

Trace choked like the idea strangled him.

She pretended great concern. "Do you need me to pat your back?"

He waved her away and shook his head, starting another bout of coughing.

"Aw. I just want to help."

"I don't think I need the kind of help you're apt to dish out," he managed to say.

She chuckled and was rewarded by an echoing giggle from Cora. Mandy turned her attention to the girl. "He sure gets all cautious at times. You think he's afraid I might hurt him?"

Cora met Mandy's eyes full-on for a moment, long enough for Mandy to see the brimming humor and take hope the girl still knew how to enjoy life. Then Cora ducked away, hiding behind the flaps of her bonnet.

"Not afraid," Trace protested. "Only realistic. After all, you have an ax in your hand. My motto is 'Never take chances with a woman wielding an ax.'"

That brought another giggle from Cora, and Mandy grinned widely at Trace. *See*, she said silently. *Isn't life better when you stop hiding?* Only she meant when Cora stopped hiding.

Trace quirked an eyebrow. Not necessarily in agreement though.

They both bent to their work until they met in the middle. Their foreheads touched. Mandy dared not continue to use her ax. Not for the reasons Trace insinuated but because her hands weren't steady. She edged back, pushed to her feet, and glanced at the sky. "Oh my. I didn't realize it's so late. I gotta go before Joanna sends someone looking for me." She jogged to the path, paused to look back and wave. "See you both tomorrow." And then she sped toward town and her worried sisters.

A few minutes later, Mandy raced by the men congregating outside the stopping house. Several of them looked startled. She didn't care if they were surprised at her haste or the fact she wore trousers. The Hamilton girls did things their way.

"Where have you been?" Joanna demanded as Mandy skidded into the dining room. "I was so worried I haven't served the meal yet."

Glory came from the kitchen to watch. "I was about to ride up the hill and drag you home."

"I'm sorry. But you'll understand when I tell you what happened." She pushed past and grinned at Glory. "Don't say a word," she whispered, then grabbed up a big bowl of potatoes and headed back to the dining room. "Let's get this bunch fed."

"I can hardly wait to hear what kind of a story you

concoct," Glory whispered as they passed again. "But it better be good."

Mandy shook her head.

She didn't get a chance to say anything further until the meal was over and the men departed outside to wait for the dining room to be cleaned up and the table pushed against the wall, creating an area in which they could spread their bedrolls. The girls used the intervening time to wash the stack of dishes.

"I'm waiting for your excuse," Joanna said as she scraped the leftovers into a bucket. Someone usually begged for scraps to feed their dog.

"I saw Cora today." She told the whole story. "I don't think her burn is that disfiguring, but she is very conscious of it."

"The poor girl," Joanna said.

Glory hooted. "I was thinking that poor man. Mandy has not given him a moment's peace since she discovered him."

Joanna and Glory looked at each other and grinned like they shared a secret.

"What?" Mandy demanded.

"We never said anything."

"I saw the way you looked." She planted her hands on her hips and gave them each her most insistent look. "You were thinking something."

Glory nodded. "But you don't want to know what it was." She bounced away, holding up her hands, ready to defend herself. She tipped her head with a come-on-I'm-ready gesture.

Mandy ignored the taunt. "I do, too."

"You're sure?"

Joanna watched the pair sparring with a look of patient endurance.

"Of course I am."

"Very well. But remember you asked for it."

Mandy grunted. What could they possibly think she'd get upset about?

"It sounds very much like you can't stay away from this Trace Owens." Glory began edging toward the door. "I think you've found a man you're interested in. Love is in the air." She ducked out the door, calling over her shoulder. "Mandy and Trace. Mandy and Trace." She raced across the yard and headed for the road, thinking she could escape.

Mandy threw the towel on the table and took off in hot pursuit. "You take that back."

She didn't catch up until they reached the little shop where Glory shoed horses. By then both were out of breath and collapsed to the step.

Finally Glory was able to speak. "Don't you think it's about time we met Trace and his sister?"

"That's a good idea. I'll see if I can persuade them to come. But I wonder if Cora will be ready to let others see her."

"Are you really beginning to care for this man?"

Mandy considered Glory's question. "He is annoying and bullheaded, but I do admire how gentle he is with his sister." She gave Glory a little shove. "People who treat younger sisters kindly can't be all bad." She shoved her harder. "Too bad you didn't realize that."

Laughing, Glory pushed back. Soon they were both giggling.

Glory glanced up. "Here comes Levi." She sprang to her feet and waited for him to reach her side.

Levi stepped close and stole a kiss in the shadow of the doorway.

Mandy groaned. "Such inappropriate behavior especially for a preacher and his fiancée. You're fortunate no one saw you."

They both looked unrepentant.

Glory chuckled. "I'll never be appropriate. Look at what I wear." She indicated her tight dungarees. "Levi loves me anyway."

"You're exactly what this preacher man needs." He took Glory's arm and the pair wandered away.

Mandy watched for a moment. Somewhere deep in the inmost parts of her heart, she felt a longing for something similar.

Like Glory said often enough, Mandy was always looking for what her pa failed to give her. Only she wasn't picturing Pa at this particular moment.

"Shoot. I must be losing my mind." She stalked back to the stopping house to help Joanna.

For some inexplicable reason, the next morning she took her time about returning to the building site. She cut down a number of trees and bundled them together to drag to her house. But still she didn't take them there.

All night she'd thought of Trace, even in her sleep. She dreamed of his gentleness and loyalty to Cora. She re-lived the way his hands felt on her shoulders, the way his eyes flashed bright blue or darkened according to his mood. The sudden awareness of something inside her she didn't know existed until now…a jolt of an emotion she couldn't name. But it seemed to have a Trace-shaped hollowness to it. Or so she'd decided in the middle of the night.

In the light of day, she decided she'd been more than slightly crazy.

But the remnants of the feeling lingered, making her uncertain how to face him.

She chewed on her lips. Mandy Hamilton never let anything upset her equilibrium. It was not about to happen now either.

Grabbing the rope, she pulled her load toward her house. Yeah, even she had a hard time calling it a *house,* but she'd never admit it. "Morning," she called, as she entered the clearing.

Only after she dropped her burden did she bother to look around.

Trace, who'd been notching a log, straightened to greet her. Did she detect the same guardedness she felt?

For some reason, the thought gave her courage. She grinned. "Hard at it still? Not ready to concede defeat yet?"

"Not a chance." He tipped his head toward the tent.

She was afraid to look. Had Cora holed up in there, prepared to sweat out the hot sunshine? When she saw Cora bent over the cooking fire, stirring a pot of something, she almost cheered. Yes, she still wore that silly poke bonnet as if it were armor, but she was outside.

Mandy sent Trace a wide smile.

He nodded, happiness wreathing his face. *"Thank you,"* he mouthed.

She tipped her head in acknowledgment. Though he might not be thanking her by the end of the day. Leaving the tent was only the first step for Cora. "Morning, Cora."

Cora glanced at her. "Hi, Mandy. You've come back to torture Trace?"

"It's the driving force of my life."

They both chuckled.

Trace groaned. "Sounds like you two plan to make my life miserable."

"Not me, dear brother." Cora pressed a hand to her heart. "Why would you think such a thing?"

He shifted his gaze to Mandy, and she simply smiled. "I've made no secret of it from the beginning, have I?"

He gave a long-suffering sigh, but he favored her with a look that was rich with amusement.

If she wasn't mistaken, he enjoyed her form of torture. "You better get to work, big bad wolf, before this little piggy finishes her twig house."

He laughed and bent to continue notching the log.

She stared as pleasure warred with a hundred cautions she'd developed over the years, and for a fleeting moment, she wondered if this was how Glory felt around Levi.

Then she realized her thoughts again bordered on foolish or worse. They weren't enemies per se, but neither were they exactly friends. In fact, she couldn't say what they were, apart from competitors in trying to establish a claim to this piece of land.

The thought straightened out her confusion immediately, and she turned her attention to building her house.

The heat grew as the day lengthened. But Trace did not slacken his pace. Neither did she.

Midday, Cora announced, "I've plenty of stew for all of us. You might as well take lunch with us, Mandy."

Mandy gratefully accepted. She was famished, hot, and thirsty.

The three of them dished up the stew and moved away from the cooking fire to eat. They chose a shady spot where a cooling breeze blessed them.

Cora carefully kept her face turned from Mandy, but at least she sat with them.

The meal finished, the three of them leaned back against the trees, Trace between Mandy and Cora.

"Where have you come from?" she asked.

The air stiffened. She didn't need to look at either to know the question made them nervous.

Then Trace eased back into an indolent position. "Missouri. We're from Missouri."

She tried to think what she knew about Missouri, but it was embarrassingly little, never having paid much attention to such things. The political discussion she'd overheard at the stopping house centered mostly on the Civil War. She couldn't imagine friend fighting against friend, or worse, brother against brother. "We sometimes see families moving West to get away from the war." She assumed they were doing the same.

Neither of them answered.

"Is it possible in Missouri to avoid being affected by the war?" Mandy asked.

Cora gave a strangled sound. Trace bolted to his feet and strode away.

"I've got a house to build."

Mandy rose more slowly, fully aware she'd said something to upset the brief spell of contentment among them. "I was only trying to make conversation."

"We know," Cora murmured. "But it's a touchy subject for us." She took the dirty dishes and hurried to clean up.

Mandy supposed she should drop the subject and promise to forget about it, but their reluctance only served to make her more curious.

The Owenses certainly had their share of secrets. And she didn't like secrets. Reminded her too much of Pa. He would have his little secrets and wouldn't tell the girls even though they knew something was up. Then one day he'd be gone. Most times with no warning. No forwarding address. No invitation to join him. They'd be left in the care of anyone he could interest in the idea.

No, she didn't like secrets one little bit.

"I was only showing a little interest in you," she muttered as she returned to her house. "It's not like I'll condemn you for what side you support." *Whack, whack*. She adjusted the supporting posts.

No answer from either Owen except for a muffled sound from Trace and a vicious swing of the ax.

He better be careful or he'd injure himself.

"I guess it has something to do with why you're here."

Trace lowered his ax to the ground, wiped his brow, and glowered at her. "Now why would you say that?"

She studied her house as if it required all her attention, but she couldn't have said what she saw. "I don't know. Intuition maybe. Or because"—she glared at him till her eyes stung— "when I mentioned the war, both of you bolted like I'd thrown scalding water on you."

He stalked over to plant himself directly before her. "Mandy Hamilton, you are the most persistent woman I've had the misfortune of meeting. Once you get an idea in that…that"—he sputtered—"that head of yours, you worry it to death like an old hound dog with a rank bone."

"My, but you do know how to sweet-talk a woman." She ground about on her heel, putting distance between them for his safety. "First a pig, and now an old hound with a smelly bone." She gave the wretched building before her careful consideration. "I wouldn't be surprised if you offended some pretty little gal back in Missouri with your sweet-talk, and she ran you out of town."

Cora, scouring dishes, giggled.

"Yes, I'm persistent," Mandy continued, her anger fueling heated words. "Let that be a warning to you, Trace Owens. Right now I've got my mind set on owning this land, and like you said, I don't give up."

She grabbed her ax and headed for the woods to find more trees. But amid her anger, Mandy felt scraped to hollow rawness. She was only trying to be friendly. Something she thought he would welcome after he'd almost hugged her yesterday.

Just went to show how far you could trust a man to have regard for your feelings. About as far as she could throw him with one hand tied behind her back. Which wasn't very far.

Trace couldn't believe only this morning he thought she was sweet and pretty. Believed he'd felt attracted to her as they stood arm to shoulder.

They worked throughout the afternoon in silence as his heart continued to vibrate with anger. Anger at the deceit of those who'd forced him into this position and made it impossible for him to trust anyone, but especially anger at Mandy with her persistent prodding. Unknowingly, she'd picked a newly formed scab off a fresh wound.

As if she had any right to stick her nose into their business. He'd never met a more annoying woman in all his born days.

It was a relief when she tossed aside her ax, called an abrupt, unfriendly good-bye, and disappeared into the woods. Finally he could take in a decent lungful of air and edge aside his anger.

Thankfully Cora kept her opinion about the whole episode to herself, though he felt her measuring look more than once.

Next morning, the events of the previous day lingered like a persistent headache. He downed two cups of coffee without relief.

Cora sat back watching him, well aware of his unsettled mood. "Why don't you tell her what happened and get it over with?"

"Because I don't trust her. Don't trust anyone."

"What's she going to do? Announce it to the whole town?"

"Maybe."

"I wonder if people here will care. Didn't Mandy say she's seen people heading West to avoid the war? Maybe they'll understand our desire to be neutral."

"I simply can't see any benefit in telling our story."

Cora shifted closer. "I am not the only one scarred by what happened."

He jerked up to stare at her, letting his gaze drift to her burn.

She brushed it with her fingertips. "I know you don't have an outward scar, but both of us have damage here." She pressed a palm to her chest. "No one can see it. But it hurts as much as anything on the outside. And makes us want to hide from people every bit as much as my face does. I understand. You don't want to open up to her because you're afraid of getting hurt again. But I don't think Mandy is like Annabelle." She settled back to cradle her cup of coffee. Then she chuckled. "She isn't anything like Annabelle."

"Good morning," Mandy sang out.

Trace stilled the surprise jolting along his nerves. How had she managed to step into their camp without him hearing her?

Because he was so busy trying not to think of her.

"Looks like it might be a little cooler today. That's good news."

Neither Trace nor Cora had answered her yet. He guessed Cora was as surprised as he at having the object of their discussion show up unexpectedly.

He glanced around. Either he'd spent a lot of time drinking coffee, or Mandy was earlier than usual.

"Trace? Cora? Is something wrong?"

He shook away his mental fog. "Good morning, Mandy."

Cora greeted her, too.

"Aren't you early today?"

She leaned back, her arms across her middle. "Got to get my house built." But she stood there grinning, not even looking toward her twig house.

What was she up to?

Her shirt billowed and wiggled.

He bolted to his feet. "Mandy, what's in your shirt?"

"Oh, that." She dug inside. "A little something for you. Not you exactly. It's for Cora." She brought forth a black-and-white ball of fur.

"A cat?"

"A kitten." She cupped it in her palms and held it out to Cora.

Cora took the kitten and cradled it to her cheek. "He's so soft." She laughed. "He's purring." Eyes shining, she looked at Mandy. "Where did you get him?"

"A man left five kittens at the stopping house. He said they were weaned now, and he didn't want to take them farther. He took the mama cat with him. Joanna picked out one to keep. Said she wouldn't mind a cat to keep the mice down. The others found new homes almost immediately. I claimed this one for you." She beamed at Trace, saw his watchfulness, shifted her attention back to Cora, and was rewarded with nothing but pleasure in Cora's expression.

"You're sure it's okay if we have him?"

Mandy nodded. "He's yours."

The cat played with the strings of Cora's bonnet.

"What did the others look like?"

Mandy hunkered down at Cora's side, teasing the kitten with a blade of grass. "Joanna kept one that is more black than white. Then there was one almost all white. This one, though, had a nice balance of both. The fourth was all mottled looking and the fifth striped."

"This is the best one of the lot then."

"I thought so. Glad you approve."

Cora favored Mandy with a smile.

Trace held his breath and waited for Cora to realize her bonnet had fallen to her shoulders and jerk it back up. Instead she dragged one ribbon toward the kitten, laughing when he caught it between his paws and growled.

"Look at that. He's a born hunter." Cora lifted her face to Trace. "Isn't he sweet?"

It wasn't the kitten he thought of. It was Cora, seemingly forgetting her burned cheek for the first time since the fire. And Mandy, who'd worked this little miracle with her gift. He squatted beside Cora and scratched the cat's head. The impossibly tiny creature grabbed his finger and licked it.

"He likes you," Cora said.

Trace didn't know if it was true, but for sure he liked what the cat had wrought in his sister's behavior. "What are you going to call him?"

Cora grew thoughtful. "I don't know. But not a silly pet name. This cat deserves a noble name."

Mandy chuckled. "He's so tiny. Why not call him Goliath?"

The three of them laughed at the idea. But Trace knew before Cora announced it. The cat was stuck with the name.

"Goliath it is," Cora said. She grew serious. "Mandy, thank you for bringing him."

Mandy draped an arm across Cora's shoulders and gave her a little hug.

Trace's throat tightened.

"You're welcome. I thought he might provide you with some company."

The teasing look she gave Trace sent a thrill through his veins. He knew she expected him to object, as if he weren't enough company for his sister. But he was too pleased with the situation to rise to her bait. In fact, he feared his eyes might reveal far too much of what he thought and felt toward Mandy at the moment. He pushed to his feet and went to work on constructing a fine log house, determined he would think of nothing else until he finished.

At that time, Mandy would leave them alone.

When had the word *alone* ever sounded so barren?

Chapter 7

Trace looked up as Mandy grabbed her ax and strode into the woods in search of more twigs. He needed to cut more trees, too, and headed the same direction. His path took him past Mandy, and his steps slowed. He dropped the reins of his horse. But still he didn't move toward her. Something inside him had shifted hard to the right at her kindness to Cora. The same feeling that shifted the opposite direction yesterday when she'd been so annoyingly persistent. In fact, he felt bruised on either side of his chest from the way his emotions bounced back and forth.

But he couldn't pass without acknowledging what she'd done for Cora. He went to her side, being careful to stay away from the swing of her ax. "Mandy?"

She rested the ax head on the ground and faced him, her expression guarded as if she expected another insult or angry retort.

To his shame, he knew she had reason for her caution.

He had not been a gentleman. And why she brought out the worst in him, he couldn't explain. But at this moment he felt nothing but goodwill toward her. "It was kind of you to bring Cora a kitten."

"You're welcome," she said, even though he hadn't exactly said the words *thank you*. "You needn't be surprised that I can be kind."

"Mandy, I'm not at all surprised."

"Really? Aren't I the most persistent, annoying person you've met? A hound and a pig?"

He hadn't said those *exact* words, but it didn't matter. He'd hurt her feelings and regretted it. He moved in cautiously, afraid of her reaction if she objected. But she only watched with guarded eyes. He grasped her shoulders simply to make sure she wouldn't attack him. Inwardly, he grinned. He knew self-defense wasn't his only motive. He wanted to touch her, feel her warmth beneath his palms. Most of all, he needed to erase the flash of pain he'd glimpsed. "Oh, Mandy. I don't mean to call you names. But you must accept there are things I cannot tell you."

She stiffened. "Secrets make me nervous."

"No need for this one to."

Her gaze searched his, reaching deep for answers, not finding all she wanted because he couldn't let her. There was a time he'd trusted a woman to hold his dreams and desires gently. He'd gone to visit her when he knew the Bushwhackers were looting in the area. He should have realized his family was in danger, but he blindly expected his friendship with Austin to protect them.

She must have seen his guardedness. "I thought you would see by now I am not your enemy, but I fear you are more cautious than Cora. She hid in a tent. You hide out in the open."

Her words were true. "I'm sorry." He dropped his hands but did not step back, struggling between a desire to hold her close and derive some comfort, and yet somehow maintain mental, emotional distance.

For several more seconds their gazes connected, searching, as the air between them shimmered with promises, hopes, and—invisible walls. He understood she could not trust him while he kept secrets. But he couldn't allow himself to break his code of silence on certain matters.

"Mandy?" The word shifted the air, breathed open a clarity between them. If things were different. If they'd met at a different time, a different place. Before life had turned sour for him.

She stepped back. "It's never mind to me what you're hiding." The way she hoisted her ax warned him she intended to get back to work. And if he was smart, he would step out of ax range.

"Thanks for your kindness to Cora."

She snorted.

He picked up the reins and moved away. Life was what it was, and he couldn't change the fact.

By the time he got back to the campsite Mandy had already returned and added another layer of branches to her—whatever it was. He couldn't dignify it by calling it a house. He dragged a log to where he needed it and stood back to admire his work. Now *this* was a house.

Mandy and Cora were both out of sight on the other side of Mandy's building. He heard shrieks of laughter; then Cora and Mandy raced around the corner, chasing Goliath. The cat ran between Trace's feet and crouched behind the log, watching for the girls.

Mandy touched Cora's arm. "Shh. You go that way, I'll go this. We'll corner him."

They tiptoed forward. The kitten picked up his ears, well aware of their every movement.

Cora crept up beside Trace. Mandy edged to the other end of the log. She nodded her head, and both sprang toward the cat. Goliath jumped over the log and darted back toward Mandy's house, Cora and Mandy in hot pursuit.

Trace leaned back and laughed heartily. Cora ignored him and continued the chase, but Mandy drew up short and faced him. She glanced toward Cora, who disappeared around the corner. Then her gaze rested on the twigs she'd dragged in.

He waited, wanting her to look at him, wanting to assure himself she held no ill will toward him. Finally, almost reluctantly, she rewarded his patience and studied him as if seeing him for the first time.

What did he want? Forgiveness? For what? For not being open with her? No, he realized. Because she was hurt by his secretiveness.

"Maybe someday," he murmured, not certain she would understand his meaning.

She flashed a smile and nodded.

His lungs expanded fully as if a weight had been yanked off his chest.

"I'm not only persistent," she said. "I'm patient."

"Nice to know." Their gaze held until he felt hope building in his heart and jerked away. "Got to finish my house." His words sounded thick.

"Yup. You get right at it. I want it as near completion as possible when I sign the deed." She laughed.

For some reason her remarks amused him. He couldn't say why, except it felt a whole lot more like they were partners than rivals.

The morning passed pleasantly enough as they worked

side by side. Again Cora invited Mandy to share their lunch, and she agreed.

"Tomorrow I'll bring something," she promised.

"Can you cook?" He tried to picture her over a stove with an apron about her waist.

"Depends what you mean by cooking." Her smile teased.

"Normally, I would mean put a pot on the stove, fill it with meat or potatoes, and cook them. Maybe put a pie in the oven."

"Well, Joanna is the pie baker. None of us can do near as well as her."

He waited. Nothing. As if that answered his question. "So you make the best"—he left plenty of time for her to insert something, anything—"uh, pudding?"

She shook her head.

"Mashed potatoes?"

A little one-shoulder shrug as if anyone could do mashed potatoes.

He looked at Cora for suggestions, but she had nothing to offer.

"Biscuits? Bread?"

"Nope."

"Then what?"

"I can turn a venison roast into the tastiest bit of meat you've ever imagined."

"Really? And how do you do that?"

She leaned forward, spoke close to his ear. "'Fraid I can't tell you. It's a secret." She leaned back, a satisfied look gleaming from her eyes. "You know how it is with secrets."

Yes, he did. And he understood she'd gained a little victory by refusing to share one with him, even though it involved nothing more important than meat.

Silently, they challenged each other. Then she grinned. "Tell you what I'll do though. I'll cook a nice big roast for you so you can see for yourself." She sprang to her feet, humming as she returned to her work.

Despite the cooler morning, the afternoon grew still and hot, forcing them to retreat to the shade several times for a break.

Cora offered to help Trace but he refused, telling her to stay away from the logs. He hated seeing the flash of hurt in her face as she backed off. Thankfully she turned her attention to the kitten and enticed it into the shade. A few minutes later Mandy and Trace flung themselves down on the grass beside Cora to cool off.

Mandy shifted to look across the valley. "I wonder if Levi and Glory are able to work."

"What are they doing?" Trace lounged back, knowing this guileless woman would share the information freely.

"I told you Levi's the preacher man Glory is going to marry. She was certainly suspicious of him to start with." She told about a sister who rode like a wild man, who shod horses and worked with the abused ones. She told of a preacher who came to town. "Glory said he dressed more like a cowboy than a preacher. But now they're crazy in love." She rolled her eyes. "I do mean crazy. They don't even mind kissing in front of others."

Trace laughed at the way she wrinkled her nose.

"They're building a mission house to care for orphans, the sick, and the elderly. As soon as they're done, they're going to get hitched, though Joanna thinks they should wait until the town builds a church."

"No church?"

"Nope. Sunday services are held outdoors. If it rains, we cram into the stopping house. Say…" She craned her neck to look at him. "You and Cora ought to come to the Sunday service and meet my family."

Cora gasped.

Trace shook his head. "'Fraid we aren't planning to go out in public now or at any time in the foreseeable future." He could see arguments building in Mandy's head. "Cora's not comfortable around others." He wasn't about to try and change her mind either. He didn't want to go to church. Didn't want to be reminded that his anger toward those who hurt him was wrong. Didn't want to be told God was in control, and he should forgive.

Mandy shifted her attention to Cora. "Cora, you should reconsider."

Cora lifted her bonnet from where it rested on her shoulders, tied it to her head, and pulled the sides close around her face.

Mandy sighed. "Forget church then. Come to the stopping house and meet my sisters. They've asked after you. I'll do my roast for Sunday dinner. How's that?"

Cora shook her head. "Trace, you go. I'll be fine here. I have Goliath to keep me company."

"I don't think that's wise." But at Mandy's expression—gentle pleading, hopeful anticipation—he added, "I'll think about it." Victory and pleasure gleamed in her eyes, and he almost regretted giving her any encouragement. She would likely take it as an open invitation to badger him into agreeing.

And yet he realized he didn't mind the idea of her trying to persuade him. Not at all.

I'll think about it. She'd make sure he did. Today was Friday. If she couldn't convince him to come and at least visit her sisters by Saturday evening, she might as well stop being Mandy.

Satisfied she'd find a way, she returned to work, finished for the day, and headed back to Bonners Ferry and her chores.

Before daylight the next day she was out in the woods with her rifle. Deer stole through the pink dawn to water at the river. She waited until most of them finished and moved away. Then, feeling the same reluctance she always did at killing such an innocent, beautiful creature, she downed a young buck. The shot echoed through the trees, sending protesting birds from the top branches. She dressed the animal, quartered it, hung the pieces from the back of her horse, and carried it back to the stopping house.

"Good." Joanna took the bounty. "We were starting to get low on meat. Have to feed the men well if we expect to keep in business."

Mandy refrained from pointing out they could serve hard beans and people would eat there because they had no other option, but she knew what Joanna meant. They had a reputation of good food to maintain. "Save a nice big roast for Sunday."

"Oh?"

"Yup. I'm expecting company." She grinned at Joanna's surprise.

"Trace and Cora?" Joanna asked.

"Yup."

Glory's arrival was announced by the pounding of horse hooves then she rushed in, her hair in disarray, smelling of horseflesh. She caught Joanna's question. "Ohh. Trace is coming to visit."

Mandy ignored her teasing grin. "I told him I cook the best venison roast in the world. So now I have to prove it."

"I'll be happy to meet them," Joanna said, turning her attention to the meat. "I'll have to can most of this to keep it from spoiling in the heat." She looked toward the river. "We need to build an ice house."

"I'll be happy to meet them, too," Glory said, grinning from ear to ear. "I can't imagine a man who can divert Mandy from pining for Pa." Her boots thudded on the floor as she crossed to scoop a dipper of water from the bucket on the cupboard and drink deeply.

"Who says he has?" But it had been days since she'd thought of Pa. It had nothing to do with Trace. She'd simply been busy.

She gave Glory a wide view of her back. "Joanna, maybe you could make a pie or two?"

Joanna jerked about from tending the meat, stared at Mandy, then a slow smile started at her eyes and edged toward her mouth. "Sure. I'll make pies. Any particular kind?"

Mandy squinted at her eldest sister. Why did she grin about nothing more than pies? Nothing special about wanting a pie for Sunday dinner. "I've always thought your dried apple pie was especially good. Probably the best you make." She turned her full attention to the task of washing breakfast dishes, though she couldn't help but overhear whispers between her sisters. Knew they talked about her, but she wouldn't give them the satisfaction of giving it any heed.

She washed the stack of dishes then grabbed a loaf of bread. "I'm going to take a lunch with me today." She sliced the entire loaf, grabbed the leftover bit of grouse from last night, and made thick sandwiches, liberally salted and peppered.

Joanna kept busy slicing venison and setting the pieces to soak in a brine solution in readiness for a hot, steamy afternoon of canning. But she spared many a glance at Mandy.

Glory made no pretense of doing anything but watching. She leaned against the table and studied every movement. "You sure must plan on being hungry."

"Cora and Trace have shared their lunch these past two days. I figure it's time for me to contribute." She reached for a syrup pail, removed the lid, and took out a handful of cookies and then another. "Don't worry, Joanna. I'll help you bake more."

"Uh-huh." Joanna sounded doubtful. "I've heard that before."

"I have helped."

"Never mind. You bring in meat and do other chores. I'm not complaining if my job is to do the cooking."

Mandy wrapped the sandwiches in brown paper, did the same for the cookies, dug a sack out of a cupboard, and settled the whole lot carefully so she wouldn't arrive with nothing but crumbs. "I'm going to work on my house."

Glory straightened. "I think I'll come along and have a look at your house. And your Trace."

"No, Glory. Please don't. Not yet." Both sisters looked at her like she'd said something foreign.

Joanna washed and dried her hands and stood before Mandy. "What's going on? We don't keep secrets among ourselves."

"No secret. I've told you everything." Except for the foolish way her heart jumped around when Trace looked at her, but Joanna didn't mean that. "You have to understand, Cora is only beginning to feel comfortable around me. I fear if I brought someone there she would retreat." Trace had no reason to hide, and yet she wondered if he wouldn't view a visitor as a betrayal on her part. "Wait until Sunday, and you'll meet them."

Joanna studied her a moment longer then finally nodded. "Until Sunday."

Mandy recognized it as a warning. She silently appealed to Glory, who would not think twice about choos-
ing a different direction than Joanna.

Glory considered her a full moment then nodded, albeit reluctantly.

Neither of her sisters liked secrets any better than she
did. What would it take to persuade Trace to open up?

She bid them farewell and headed up the trail to her
house. Only it wasn't her twig shack she pictured, it was
the fine log house Trace built.

Trace was missing when she arrived. Cora played with
the kitten and glanced up. "Trace has gone for another
log. He's been working since dawn."

The walls were higher than when Mandy left yesterday. He was determined to win. She left the lunch in a
shady spot to keep cool and grabbed her ax. She would
never let him beat her.

They passed each other coming and going, pausing
only long enough to say hello, even though she wanted
so much more. But at a loss to say what she thought she
wanted, she merely nodded and continued on her way.

All morning she worked. Steadily the walls grew
higher. At noon, she retrieved the lunch sack. "Time to
eat. Come and get it."

Trace washed, filled the dipper from the bucket, drank
deeply, and dumped water over his head. Then he shook
like a dog after a dip.

She watched shining droplets cling to the ends of his
hair. One ran down his cheek. He dashed it away.

Their gazes caught and held. She swallowed back a
thousand unnamed emotions clogging her throat, thick-
ening her thoughts until they were immobile. In the back

of her brain she ordered herself to stop staring open-mouthed. Stop embarrassing herself. But she lacked the power to do so.

Cora dashed between them, chasing little Goliath and freeing Mandy from her foolishness. Mandy's fingers felt thick as sausages as she handed out sandwiches, barely able to refrain from jerking back like an idiot when Trace's fingers brushed hers.

What was wrong with her? Was she sick with something? But apart from these occasional lapses of good sense, she felt fine.

Trace settled back against a tree, and she relaxed inch by inch. After a bit, the quiet heat calmed her brain, and she recalled her plan. "You know that venison roast I mentioned?"

"You mean the one you're famous for cooking?"

"Yup. Well it's definitely on the menu for Sunday dinner. This is your chance to see if it's as good as I say. Join us for the afternoon."

Cora, who had been distracted by feeding the cat bits of her sandwich, jerked her attention to Trace. "Go."

"I might."

Mandy dared not look at him. Didn't want to know if he appeared reluctant or pleased about the prospect. It was enough that he considered it. But despite her resolve, she slid a glance at him.

He watched her, his gaze steady, searching. She let him see a welcome and maybe more, though she couldn't imagine what more he'd want from her. Or what more she could offer.

With an effort she pulled her gaze away and settled it on Cora. "You ought to come, too."

"No. I couldn't." She touched her scarred cheek.

"Cora, only my sisters and Levi will be there, and they won't care about your cheek."

Cora ducked her head. "I couldn't."

"Maybe next time." She returned her attention to Trace, wondering if he felt the same promise in the words as she did.

Not giving him a chance to change his mind about coming, she handed out cookies.

"You make these?" Trace asked.

"Joanna did, but I promised her I'd do some baking." Right then and there she decided she would bake cookies at the first opportunity so she could hand some to Trace and say she'd made them.

Trace studied his face in the tiny mirror. Shaved, his hair combed back, he looked his very best. But what did Mandy see? A man with a secret, certainly. But did she see the man he'd once been? A man with normal hopes and aspirations? He touched the edges of his damp hair. Maybe he should get Cora to trim the ends. He jerked his hands from his head. Why had he agreed to go to the stopping house for dinner? "I should have told her I changed my mind."

Cora peered over his shoulder, checking his every move, pointing out a missed whisker, an untidy bit of hair. "Can't see any reason why you would."

He faced her. "I don't like leaving you alone."

"You aren't. I have Goliath with me."

"Some protection that is."

"If I hear anyone approaching, I'll slip away and hide." She patted his arm as if he needed reassuring. "Don't worry. I'll be fine. Besides, don't you think it's time you met Mandy's family?"

"Why?"

"Seems the next logical step."

"To what?"

She chuckled softly. "Your growing fondness for her."

"Fondness?" He sputtered. "How can you say that? All we do is fight. Or at least spar. So far we haven't resorted to fisticuffs. Or gunfights." Though their first meeting had involved him wrestling her to the ground. But then he didn't know she was a woman, so he could be excused.

"You're both dancing around what you feel. Not quite certain if it's real. Or if you want it to be. I think she is as cautious as you about letting herself care about someone. But she is sweet, don't you think?"

"No. She's anything but. Try sharp, annoying—"

"Once the two of you decide to trust each other, that will all be nothing."

"Cora, you're sixteen years old. I hardly think that qualifies you as an expert on romance."

"Almost seventeen, dear brother. And I don't have to be an expert to see what's right in front of me." She patted his arm in a motherly gesture that made him want to gnash his teeth. "Now you go meet her family and make a good impression."

He slammed his hat on his head, but his anger had already burned itself out. "I won't stay long so—"

"I am not worried. I am not afraid. Bye."

He paused to kiss her cheek and pat Goliath on the head. "Take care of her," he murmured to the cat. But as he strode down the path toward town, he fought his doubts. Having Cora turn this into—what? Romance? Well, what did he think it would be? A business meeting?

No. He knew it was more. But he couldn't say what. Or if he welcomed more. All he knew was he longed to know about Mandy Hamilton.

He approached the town as the ferry crossed the river

with men and horses on board. More prospectors seeking gold in the Kootenais. He had no such aspirations. All he wanted was peace and solitude.

He chuckled. Mandy had made both impossible, but he found he didn't object.

This being the first trip to Bonners Ferry since he'd passed through on his arrival, he glanced about. The typical frontier town, thrown up in haste with little preplanning. The houses and businesses clustered close to the river were built on stilts, indicating the problem of spring flooding. Other buildings higher up the hill seemed safe from the threat. The stopping house sat solidly above the marsh area. He paused to consider what he was about to do.

Meet Mandy's family. Risk people knowing of his presence. Unintentionally inviting them to visit as western people were wont to do by way of hospitality. Cora did not want company. Nor did he. Company meant friendships. Friendships were not to be trusted.

He reminded himself he would see only Mandy's family.

Perhaps it was worth the risk.

He adjusted his hat and crossed the last few hundred yards to the stopping house. He'd soon find out if this was a mistake or not.

Chapter 8

"Thought you might put on a dress," Glory said. "In honor of this occasion."

Mandy pretended she needed to put a spoon in the wash basin. At the same time she glanced out the window to see if Trace headed down the path. She'd never admit she'd wondered if he'd look at her differently if she'd found a dress and worn it. "You're going to marry a preacher. Shouldn't you start wearing dresses?" She carried a jug of water to the table.

Glory snorted. "Can't work with my horses in skirts and petticoats."

Mandy hesitated, trying to come up with an excuse to return to the window. She failed to find one so simply walked over and looked out. Still no sign of Trace.

Glory laughed. "You can hardly wait to see him again." She danced around on the floor. "Mandy and Trace. Mandy and Trace."

Rather than give her sister reason to tease, Mandy forced herself to stay away from the window. So she didn't see Trace approach.

"Here he comes," Glory called, all triumphant because she'd seen him first.

Mandy took her time about going to the window. Took too long. He'd almost reached the house, so she missed her chance to assess his attitude as he approached. Was he eager or reluctant? Or somewhere in between? It didn't matter. The important thing was he'd come.

She moseyed toward the entrance, determined no one would guess she longed to run and pull him inside before he changed his mind.

"Maybe I'll get the door," Glory said, taking two hurried strides that direction.

"Glory, stop teasing her," Joanna murmured.

"Can't. It's too much fun."

Levi chuckled. "Not to mention it would feel too much like defeat if you stopped."

Glory laughed. "She wouldn't know what to do if I didn't tease her, would you, Mandy?"

"I might be willing to find out. Just don't get carried away with Trace here."

"Oh, I'll be very good. I promise."

"Is that even possible?" By the time she opened the door, Trace had his hand raised to knock. "Hello. Come in." Her voice sound high and thin. Thankfully Glory didn't point it out to everyone present.

Trace stepped over the threshold, jerked off his hat, and stood there.

Mandy pointed to the row of hooks, and he hung his hat. She waved him toward the kitchen where the others waited. "My sisters, Joanna and Glory, and Levi, the preacher."

He shook hands all around.

"Welcome. It's nice to have another man present," Levi said.

Joanna and Glory measured him discreetly but thoroughly.

What had she expected? Of course they would. Just like she'd made her own personal assessment of Levi before she was prepared to let him befriend Glory. Ironically, both she and Joanna saw how things were between the pair before Glory did.

Her thoughts stuttered. Did they see something she didn't? It wasn't possible. Her cheeks burned to know her sisters might think so.

Joanna invited them all to sit at the smaller kitchen table, and in the ensuing shuffle she forgot the question.

Joanna indicated she and Trace should sit on one side of the table, Glory and Levi across from them. Joanna sat at the end. The food was ready and waiting. Mandy's sisters must have placed it on the table while she invited Trace in.

Joanna nodded in Levi's direction. "Would you say the blessing, please?"

Levi stood as he prayed.

They passed the food—mashed potatoes, gravy, cooked carrots, and succulent roast venison.

Trace tasted the meat and sighed. "You're right. It's delicious."

"Best you've ever tasted?"

"Think so. How do you do it?"

"It's a secret." She felt him stiffen and knew he'd caught the little emphasis on the final word. Yes, it was silly and probably childish to keep harping on the subject of secrets, but she couldn't stop herself.

"I see. An old family secret, I suppose."

Glory laughed. "She doesn't even want us to know, though all we have to do is watch her. It's something she learned from an old man who showed her how to cut up a deer."

"Took a little practice to get it perfected." In truth it wasn't that difficult. She soaked the meat in a brine solution, seared it, and rubbed a mixture of herbs and spices into it. The old trapper had told her his mixture, but she had experimented and created her own special blend.

Glory leaned toward Trace.

Mandy didn't like the look in her sister's eyes and knew she was up to no good. She reached out her foot under the table and nudged Glory's leg, but her sister ignored the warning.

"Mandy tells me the two of you are in a race to see who will get that piece of land. Tell me why you don't leave her have it and find another piece. Seems it would be a lot less trouble."

Trace's laugh rang with wry amusement. "At first, I only saw it as a challenge. Not a very tough one either, I figured in my innocence. I realize now it would have been a lot easier to walk away, but now I have a house started. A very nice log house. In fact…"

Mandy's heart sank. She should have warned him not to call hers a twig house and mention the three pigs. It was too late. All she could hope for was to change the subject. "He should have known I wouldn't be bested when I outshot him in a little contest we had."

Levi chuckled. "They're called the Buffalo Gals for a good reason."

Mandy groaned. Even Joanna looked like she wanted to stuff something into Levi's mouth to shut him up. But Glory grinned.

Trace rose to the bait as nicely as a river trout. "Buffalo Gals?"

"Yes, indeed. A well-earned title." Levi's gaze adored Glory. "It started when they trailed after their father. When they asked if people had seen him, one man asked if they meant the buffalo hunter. That's when people started calling them the Buffalo Gals. But they rightly earned the name. They wear pants, they look tough, and they are. There's nothing these three won't try and succeed in doing."

Mandy shifted a little so she could see Trace's reaction without looking directly at him.

His eyes found hers and wouldn't let her go. "I have seen it firsthand with Mandy." His grin didn't mock her. In fact—her breath caught midway up her chest and refused to budge—she could almost think his gaze was as admiring as Levi's.

No reason it should be.

But at least he didn't mention her twig house.

Levi finished his meal and pushed away his plate. He'd seen the pies and no doubt decided to save some room for a slice. "How is your house coming?"

Determined to prevent Trace from repeating some of the things he said about her construction work, she answered first. "The walls on my house are five feet high or so."

"Yes, indeed, the walls of her house are coming along quickly. Keeps me hopping to stay ahead." Trace, bless his heart, laughed—a sound so full of mocking Mandy expected everyone at the table would wonder what was so funny.

Glory leaned forward. "She can cut logs and place them as fast as you?" She shot Mandy a look of pure disbelief.

"Why should that surprise you?" Mandy demanded.

Glory shrugged. "For one thing, you aren't all that great with an ax. Joanna asks me to chop the wood for a very good reason. So either you have improved a great deal or"—she shifted her gaze to Trace—"you aren't a skilled axman." She ran her gaze up and down his arms and across his shoulders. "Something I would find hard to believe." She leaned back and crossed her arms across her chest. "I think you aren't telling the whole truth."

"Sure sounds like you're calling me a liar." Mandy jerked forward, reaching across the table toward Glory, who simply backed away with a wicked grin.

"Girls," Joanna chided. "Please remember this is Sunday, and we have guests."

Levi chuckled. "Don't let our presence interfere with a little family discussion." He turned to Trace. "I've learned to stay out of their arguments and as far away as possible."

Both Glory and Mandy settled back in their chairs. Glory continued to grin while Mandy scowled.

When Glory turned her attention to Trace, Mandy guessed her sister didn't intend to heed her silent warning.

"So what is the whole truth and nothing but the truth about these houses?"

Trace spared Mandy a quick glance, but she didn't look his way to see if he intended to throw caution to the wind or guard his tongue.

"Well," he began slowly. "There is something unique about Mandy's house. You see…" He had the full attention of everyone around the table. "Mine is a fine log house that will stand for years. I intend to add on to it once I've completed the terms of our agreement and have the deed to the land."

"But what will you do with two houses?" Joanna asked.

Under the table, Mandy kicked Trace's ankle, which only brought a chuckle from his traitorous lips.

"Mandy's house will be a perfect storage shed." His demanding gaze informed her he'd been as kind as possible.

But Glory wasn't about to let it go. Talk about a hound dog with a smelly bone. Her sister qualified far more than Mandy. "You said there was something unique about her house. What?"

Trace hesitated.

Mandy tried to kick his ankle again, but he'd shifted his legs out of her reach.

"Maybe you'd like to tell them yourself?"

If looks could do damage, his cheek would be as scarred as Cora's. "Don't think so." She knew Glory would not be satisfied with that. Nor Joanna, though *she* would wait until they were alone to turn the thumbscrews.

Glory shrugged as if it didn't matter.

Her pretended indifference made Mandy's nerves twitch. What was she up to?

She didn't have to wait long to find out.

"I don't need anyone to tell me. All I have to do is walk up the trail and see for myself. In fact, I don't know why I haven't done so already."

Trace jerked halfway to his feet then subsided. "I'd like to ask you to respect our privacy."

"Mandy told us about Cora. I won't bother her. Won't even let her know I was there."

Mandy lifted her palms toward the roof in surrender. "If you must know, Miss Nosy, my house is built of—" She struggled for the right word. One that sounded better than—

"Twigs," Trace supplied.

"Twigs?" Glory hooted. "How are you keeping them stacked? With fence posts?"

"It's not twigs. It's small trees, and I'm putting them up in the same fashion Trace is using to build with thick logs." She sounded every bit as aggrieved as she felt and wanted Glory to know it. No reason to inform them she'd had to drive some poles in upright to hold her logs in place.

"It will be a perfect storage shed," Trace soothed.

The way he patted her arm and spoke so kindly did nothing to ease her anger.

Joanna, seeing Mandy's expression, tried to change the subject. "Levi, that was an excellent sermon." She shifted her gaze to Trace. "Too bad you missed it. It was about Jesus calming the winds and the waves on the sea." She returned her attention to Levi. "I like how you reminded us that God is in control of nature."

Glory tore her gaze from Mandy to Levi, and her expression changed from teasing to pure adoration so fast Mandy blinked to assure herself she wasn't seeing a mirage.

"What was that you said about the water in the ocean?" Glory asked.

"All the water in the ocean cannot sink a ship unless it gets inside." His look included everyone at the table. "All the trouble in the world cannot harm us unless it gets into our spirit."

Trace had been enjoying the teasing between Mandy and her sister. He'd been silently pleased when Mandy nudged his ankle. Okay, it was more than a nudge. More like a sharp kick. He'd have a bruise, but Levi's words brought Trace back to reality with a thud that hurt his head. Certainly he'd been taught to believe God was in control. He'd even believed it at one time. But then he realized how truly awful life could be. If God was in control of those things, then God couldn't be loving and kind, as he'd once believed.

Levi continued to speak. "Bad things happen. There is evil in the world because of sin. But faith enables each of us to rest in God's care."

Pat answers. Easy for a preacher. For a person who likely knew nothing of the sort of evil Trace had witnessed firsthand. Lies. Theft. Arson. Murder.

Joanna glanced around the table. "Anyone for a second piece of pie?"

Trace would gladly have taken another but didn't want to seem greedy. However, when Levi handed his plate forward, he did the same, thanking Joanna.

Suddenly Glory leaned forward so far she almost upset her chair. "That's why you wanted to know about the three little pigs."

Uh-oh. He couldn't imagine Mandy letting this go unchallenged. "This is really good pie, Joanna. I haven't had pie in so long I almost forgot what a treat it is."

"He said you built a house of twigs—like one of the three pigs—didn't he?"

Mandy didn't answer, but her glower was enough to tear strips from Glory's flesh, though Glory seemed unaware of her danger. She turned her burning interest to Trace.

He ducked and wished he had more pie to concentrate on, but he'd eaten the last bit and had to settle for scraping together a few flakes of pastry.

"You said that, didn't you?" Glory persisted.

He shrugged. Allowed himself one quick glance at Mandy. She studiously avoided looking at him.

"I know you did." Glory leaned toward him. "And she

let you live? Amazing." She tapped her finger on her chin. "Or maybe not." She grinned at Mandy. "Maybe not so strange at all."

Levi draped an arm across Glory's shoulders. "Give your sister some peace."

Trace wondered if Glory knew the meaning of the word. He began to feel sympathy for Mandy. No wonder she was always so ready to defend herself. Seems she'd have little choice around Glory.

But before either girl could take the conflict to another level, someone threw open the door. "Fire. Up at the Murray house. Hurry. We need all the help we can get."

Fire! Trace couldn't breathe.

Mandy and the others bolted for the door. She paused, saw him frozen in place. "Trace, aren't you going to help?"

"I'll be there." He was hot on her heels in a matter of seconds. Time was of the essence in rescuing the inhabitants and saving their belongings.

The group raced toward the center of town. Smoke billowed behind the lawyer's office. Flames shot from the window of a small house—hungry, angry flames. Consuming.

A bucket brigade formed under the shouted orders of a large man. Mandy fell in line, Glory at her elbow, then Levi and Joanna. Trace raced past and stopped before the man in charge. "Is everyone out?"

"Don't know."

Trace stared into the flames, holding up a hand to protect his face from the heat, and cocked his head. Did he hear a call for help? He moved closer to the house.

Mandy appeared at his side. "What are you doing?"

"I have to make certain there's no one inside." He inched forward, but the heat was intense.

Mandy grabbed his arm. "No, you can't go in there. You'll die."

"I can't stand by and not do something. Listen. Do you hear that?"

"How can you hear anything but people yelling and the flames crackling? It's not possible. Trace, you aren't thinking right."

He tore away from her grasp and raced around to the other side of the house. There had to be another door. A window. Mandy followed him. "I'm going in." He grabbed a rock and broke the glass. Hot air whooshed out.

"Trace, no. It's too dangerous." But she turned, hearing the same thing he did. A call for help.

"I must." He used the rock to remove the sharp fragments of glass in the frame then swung his leg through the hole. "Wait here."

"If you're going in there, so am I."

He reached through the window and grabbed her shoulders. Shook her hard. "Do as I say. Stay there."

He recognized the stubborn set of her chin. "Please, Mandy. I couldn't bear it if you got burned." A thousand pictures filled his mind. The fire that had destroyed his home. Killed his parents, Cora screaming as he pulled her from the flames. "Please wait." He dropped his hand. He must get to that voice. He crouched low and pushed into the smoke and heat.

He made his way through the room, following the call for help, reached a doorway, and paused. The fire raged to his left, sizzling angrily as bucket after bucket of water reached it. For a moment, the flames died back as if beaten then roared to life again. He turned to his right, down a hall. Through the smoke he made out another doorway and crept through it.

"Help me." A woman saw him, grabbed an arm, and dragged him forward. "My husband. He isn't moving."

A man lay on the floor.

"What happened?"

"He fell. Banged his head on the dresser."

Trace grabbed the unconscious man's shoulders and, keeping low, dragged him toward the door.

The woman whimpered, rooted to the floor.

"Follow me. I'll get you out."

She moaned, but her feet didn't leave the spot.

"Lady, we have to get out."

"I'll get her." Mandy crawled past him, pulled the woman to her knees, and pushed her toward the doorway.

"I told you to stay."

"I never agreed, did I?"

He pulled the man; she pushed the woman until they were back near the window. He wanted to be angry at Mandy, but he couldn't. All that mattered was getting the four of them out safely. Someone jumped through the window and grabbed the injured man. Many hands reached forward to take him.

Mandy pushed the woman forward, and hands pulled her to safety.

The heat grew intense, the smoke so thick Trace's eyes streamed with tears. Between the tears and the smoke he couldn't see Mandy. Couldn't see the window. "Mandy," he rasped. "Where are you?"

She coughed. Couldn't stop.

He reached out. Connected with her arm. Dragged her to where he knew the window had to be. Flames licked overhead, crackling like the laughter of the devil. "Get out." He didn't let go of her arm until he felt another hand, heard a voice saying, "We got you." The hands ripped her from his grasp.

The noise overhead roared. Flames surrounded him. He coughed, choking. His eyes streamed.

Then everything went black.

Chapter 9

Mandy stared up into the sky, her lungs searing from the smoke she'd inhaled. Joanna bent over her on one side, Glory on the other.

Joanna's hands examined her, stroked her hair. "You'll survive."

"I know you're crazy," Glory said, her voice heavy with concern despite the anger she tried to convey. "But I never thought I'd see you dive into a burning building."

Mandy gasped, tried to speak but discovered her voice had disappeared in the pain of a burned throat. She reached for Joanna's shirt front and pulled her close, barely able to focus through the sting of her eyes. "Trace?" She mouthed the word. "Is Trace okay?"

"He's fine." Joanna was the world's worst liar.

Trace wasn't fine. Panic stole her strength, and she lay like an old rag. But she must find him. She tried to sit up.

Got as far as one elbow. Ignored her dizziness, her seared throat, her ineffectual lungs.

Where is he? She begged Joanna silently.

Joanna nodded to a group of men beyond them.

Help me. She appealed to both sisters.

Joanna and Glory exchanged a look.

"I know how I'd feel if it were Levi," Glory said, and pulled her to her feet. She'd have never made it without their help. With a sister on either side, Mandy stumbled through the men.

The men parted. Trace lay on the ground.

"Trace." The groaned word ripped her frightened heart every bit as cruelly as it scraped up her damaged throat.

She jerked from her sisters' arms and fell to her knees beside Trace's inert body. With arms so weak and trembling she didn't recognize them as her own, she pressed palms to his chest. A cry of relief escaped when she felt it rise. He was alive.

She leaned over, pressed her face to his smoke-streaked shirt front, and cried. She hoped everyone would think her eyes were streaming from the smoke.

Hands pulled her back, and she collapsed to the ground, one hand clinging to Trace's as he lay motionless at her side. Motionless except for the rise and fall of his chest.

She coughed again and again. Joanna eased her to her side.

"Cough it all out."

Like she could stop. She coughed until she wondered her lungs didn't come out. She drank cupful after cupful of water.

In the meantime, several people hovered around Trace, discussing what they should do.

"He got clunked on the head when the beam came down. He needs to lie still until he comes to."

"No," another "expert" said, "he needs to hang his head over a bench or something to clear his lungs."

"My old granny said there wasn't nothing that couldn't be fixed with a good dose of salts."

Mandy met Joanna's gaze and rolled her eyes.

Joanna chuckled. "Sounds like Mrs. Ester."

Mandy nodded. They'd once been left in the care of a woman who treated everything from cough to tummy ache to tardiness with a dose of salts. The girls had quickly learned nothing hurt as much as the result of that particular medication and never complained about any ache or discomfort.

Bull, from the saloon, joined the circle, a bottle in his hand. "A snort of whisky will set him right."

One of the men jeered. "He can't swallow when he's out cold."

Feeling a little stronger, Mandy edged to Trace's side. She managed to whisper his name. She stroked his cheek, streaking the smoky smudges. She breathed a silent plea. *Trace. Don't die on me. Not just when I discover how much you mean to me. Please, God. Don't let him die.*

Levi pushed aside the men and knelt at Trace's side. He gave him careful consideration then reached for Mandy's hand. Glory joined him and took her other hand. Joanna stood behind her and rested her palms on Mandy's shoulders. Then Levi prayed. "Father in heaven, we ask for the life of this good man. He's saved others. Please save him."

"Are Mr. and Mrs. Murray okay?" Mandy whispered.

Levi answered her. "Mr. Murray has a lump on his head, but they'll be just fine. Thanks to you and Trace."

"It's thanks to Trace. He was certain he heard someone. I only followed him in to make sure he got out safely." It hurt to talk even at a whisper, but everyone needed to know Trace was a hero.

She couldn't take her eyes off his still face. Even streaked and dirty, his was the most handsome face she'd ever seen. Why had she wasted their time together fighting with him? What if she didn't get a second chance?

His eyes fluttered.

"Trace." She wanted to hug him and kiss him.

He coughed, gasping for air. Levi sat him up as he coughed out the smoke in his lungs.

Trace pushed Levi's steadying hands away. Jerked about as if seeking something. His gaze rested on Mandy. He stopped searching and reached for her hand.

"You're safe." The words croaked from him.

"I'm safe. The Murrays are safe. And you're a hero."

"No hero," he managed. "Is the fire out?"

"Dowsed, and nothing else affected."

He nodded, and with a strangled moan, reached for his head.

"The roof came down on you," Levi said.

A crowd gathered 'round to see for themselves the man who'd risked his life to save Mr. and Mrs. Murray.

"Who is he?"

"Where did he come from?"

"What's your name, mister?"

Mandy turned to Levi and spoke quietly. "He doesn't want people to know he lives here. He thinks he has to protect Cora." For now they wouldn't argue about whether or not he was right.

Levi nodded and got to his feet. "Folks, give the man a chance to rest. His name is Trace, and he was visiting at the stopping house."

Trace relaxed visibly.

Mandy realized she clung to Trace's hand and jerked away.

Levi signaled to a couple of men. "Let's get these people to the stopping house to rest."

Joanna and Glory helped Mandy to her feet. She shook off their assistance. "I can walk on my own." And she hurried to Trace's side, hovering close to make sure he didn't fall as Levi and another man half carried him to the stopping house.

Joanna dashed ahead to set up a cot for Trace by the time they arrived.

Trace shook off helping hands and refused to accept the comfort of the narrow bed. "I must get back."

But it was obvious he was too weak.

Mandy knew that fact wouldn't deter him. "I'll go to Cora and explain what happened. You better not leave while there are so many people milling about. Unless you want someone following you." She stared into his eyes, hoping he might reconsider his need to hide. Cora's desire to hide.

But he only nodded.

She wondered how long he could continue to conceal his whereabouts. People weren't stupid, and if they wanted to find him for any reason, good or otherwise, they would. But now was not the time to discuss differences of opinion. "I'm not leaving until I see you on that cot."

They dueled with their gazes, his rapier sharp despite the smoke and streaks on his skin.

"And wash your face."

He chuckled. "Maybe you should look in a mirror."

She dashed to the mirror in the bedroom and groaned. She looked down. Her clothes were as soiled as her skin. She went to the kitchen and washed her face and hands then ducked into the bedroom and slipped into a clean shirt and trousers.

When she stepped into the big dining room, Trace lay stretched out on the cot, an arm thrown across his eyes. He shifted his arm so he could watch her. Grinned at her clean clothes. "That's better."

"Can't say the same for you."

"I'll have to wait until I return to camp." His voice was hoarse. He had to pause to catch his breath. "Tell Cora I'm safe. Tell her—"

"I'll tell her the truth."

"Don't frighten her."

Feeling sorry for his predicament, she crossed the room and squatted at his side. "Trace, trust me to take care of this little thing."

He reached for her hand. "I know you don't agree, but promise me you'll keep Cora's whereabouts a secret."

She examined their joined hands. Allowed herself to likewise examine her feelings. She cared about him enough to accept his way of thinking on this subject even though she thought he was mistaken. She would do as he asked even though it was in her power to choose whatever direction she wanted. However, when she tackled the situation she would do so openly. No sneaking around doing things behind his back. "No one will know where I've gone. You can count on that."

"Thank you." He squeezed her hand. "For everything."

"Everything? I'm only making one promise." She didn't want him to get the idea she vowed eternal silence on anything.

"For being you."

His words fell into her heart with a sweetness that stung her eyes and threatened to make her start coughing again. "I best be going." She slipped her hand free from his grasp and headed for the door without a backward look. If she looked at him—saw the tenderness she hoped and feared she'd see—she would embarrass herself by weeping.

Sneaking away from the stopping house was no problem. Any more than taking a roundabout trail through the woods that left no clue of her passing.

She approached the camp in silence and looked around for Cora. At first she didn't see her; then she heard a whisper and detected a movement up the hill in some underbrush. She caught a flash of black and white as Goliath chased something. Cora was hiding there, but the kitten gave away her position.

Mandy straightened and walked into the camp as if everything was normal. "Cora? Where are you? It's me."

Cora scampered from the bushes, scooping up Goliath as she descended the hill. She was five feet from Mandy before she glanced up and looked past Mandy. "Where's Trace?"

"He'll be along later."

Mandy's face wrinkled into a map of worry. "Why isn't he here now?"

"He's resting."

Cora cried out. "What happened?"

"Come, sit down, and I'll explain everything." She led the girl over to the log house and pulled her down to sit side by side with their backs against the wall. "Trace is a hero."

Cora nodded. "I know."

Mandy smiled. Of course he was a hero to his sister. "Because of him two people are alive today."

"Two? But..." She turned to study Mandy. "I meant when he rescued me. But we aren't talking about the same thing, are we?"

It would be interesting to know the details behind Cora's words. "There was a fire in town today."

"A fire?" Cora pressed the cat to her chest with both hands. Little Goliath seemed to sense his job was to provide comfort and didn't protest.

"He insisted on going into the burning house and helping the two occupants escape. He took in a lot of smoke and got a bang on the head, but he's okay."

Cora moaned.

Mandy rushed out the last words. "He's resting for now." She didn't say Trace would find it impossible to leave without one of the curious or grateful following him.

Cora rocked back and forth. "Poor Trace. Poor Trace."

Mandy reached for Cora's arm, trying to still the frantic movement. "He's okay."

Cora turned wide-eyed shock toward her. "But it will remind him of everything." She touched her cheek. Her face crumpled, and a sob shook her.

Mandy pulled the girl to her and patted her back. "He was very brave."

"He always is. Our parents were killed in a house fire. He tried to save them, but they were already gone. He pulled me from the flames." Every word was punctuated with a sob. "I don't know if he'll ever stop blaming himself."

"Why should he blame himself?"

"He just does." Cora wailed and clutched Mandy's arms, squeezing Goliath between them. The cat meowed a protest and wriggled free to sit at Cora's knees and groom himself.

Cora quieted then sat up. "You're sure he's okay?"

"I wouldn't have left if I wasn't."

Cora nodded. "He protects me by keeping us hidden.

I appreciate it. I don't want people to stare at me and call me horrible names."

Mandy squeezed Cora's arm. "You need to give people a chance to see past your burn to your sweetness."

Cora watched the cat. "Trace is hiding as much as I am, you know."

"What's he hiding from?"

"People."

"But why?"

Cora grew still. Stared into the distance, past the trees, past the present. "People are not always who you think they are. Sometimes friends turn out to be enemies. How do you know who to trust?"

"Someone turned against him?"

"Friends, supposedly. A good lesson not to trust anyone."

The blanket decision stung like hot smoke. It seared right to the pit of her stomach. "You don't trust me?"

Cora gave her a crooked smile. "You're the exception."

Mandy knew her smile was equally uncertain. She didn't want to be the only exception. There were plenty of good, decent people out there if only Trace would give them a chance. Surely he'd seen that today. First, at the stopping house where only good honest people sat around the table then later, when many hands had dealt with the fire and many people had expressed concern and gratitude for Trace.

Cora picked up the kitten and moved to the edge of the clearing. She picked up a basket of mending and examined a tear in one of Trace's shirts.

Mandy knew the chance to press for more information or to suggest a flaw in her thinking had passed…for now.

"When will he be back?" Cora asked.

"I don't think it would hurt him any to spend the night. I'll stay until he returns."

She leaned back to watch Cora, who kept her attention on threading a needle. For the first time since Mandy had been pulled from the burning building, she had a chance to examine her feelings. To admit without pressure or fear that she had grown fond of Trace. Extremely fond. Now what did she intend to do about it? She shifted to study her twig house. If she really wanted to, she could finish the house in a matter of days—hours, even.

The question was—did she want to beat Trace? Did she want to take the land from him? Would he leave if she did?

She sprang to her feet and circled her house and then the one Trace built. Her thoughts raced ahead as she worked out a plan.

Trace slept in restless fits, waking often to cough. His lungs burned. His head felt like a beam had landed on it. Which was exactly what happened, according to Levi.

Glory and Joanna bustled about the kitchen. Men mingled outside, waiting for the meal to be served.

Trace pushed himself to the side of the cot, sat until the dizziness passed, then made it to his feet.

Joanna noticed and hurried from the kitchen. "You need to rest."

"I'm not going to lie here in the middle of the room and be an object of interest while those men come in to eat. Thank you for the meal and for your kindness in providing me a place to rest, but I'll be heading on home now."

Joanna gave him serious study. "You're sure you can make it on your own? Glory could help you."

He held up a protesting hand. The movement caused

his head to pound, and he choked back a groan. "No need."

"Very well."

Glory joined her sister in the doorway. "Sure wouldn't want to be in your shoes if you collapse on the trail and Mandy finds you."

"I can handle anything Mandy hands out."

Joanna and Glory laughed.

He smiled weakly. "Maybe not at the moment though." He stepped out to the porch and went to a washbasin to clean up.

Two men moved in to shake Trace's hand and thank him for helping fight the fire. But the majority of them were simply passing through. Many weren't even aware there'd been a fire. He made his way to the edge of the yard and leaned against a shed as if waiting with the others for supper to be announced.

Finally, Joanna came to the door and rang a cowbell suspended on a hook, signaling mealtime. They paused at her side to drop coins into the can she held. Trace hung back, and when the last man stood before her, he ducked out of sight and headed up the trail. He paused several times to let his heartbeat slow to normal and to listen for anyone following him. Satisfied he had no company, he did his best to hurry onward.

A few feet from the clearing he stopped and listened. The girls laughed. Perhaps playing with Goliath.

Then Cora screamed.

He charged into the clearing. "What's wrong?"

Cora and Mandy stared at him with wide eyes.

"Goliath scratched me," Cora said. "Trace, you look awful."

Mandy rushed to his side. "You better sit down."

"I'm fine." But he let her lead him to their usual spot and gladly sank to the ground.

Cora hung over him. "For a hero you look pretty grubby."

"You should have seen me before I cleaned up."

"I can't believe you went into a burning building." She sat facing him, her knees drawn up, her brow knotted. "You could have been burned." She pressed her palm to her cheek.

He hadn't stopped to consider the risks. He'd simply acted. Determined not to let a fire claim another life. Or two. But now he realized how close he'd come to dying. How close Mandy had come. His gaze sought and found Mandy's. "You were supposed to wait outside. Where it was safe."

Cora gasped. "You went in, too. Why would you?"

Mandy's gaze held Trace's like a vise. "I had to make sure Trace was okay."

The sound coming from Cora's mouth rang with disbelief and likely a lot of fear. "I can't believe either of you. If something happened…"

She grabbed the ever-present kitten and stalked up the hill to the thicket, where she disappeared.

Trace continued to drown in Mandy's look. He remembered the moment when he'd regained his senses. "I thought you were gone." His voice grated as he recalled that initial fear. He touched her cheek, assuring himself that she was, indeed, okay.

She pressed her hand to his, keeping his fingers against her warm skin. "I thought the same thing about you. You gave me quite a scare." She shook her head back and forth. "After Cora told me your parents died in a fire, I found it impossible to believe you would dash in to rescue strangers."

"She told you about our parents?" He withdrew his hand and shifted his gaze. How much had Cora revealed?

Mandy nodded. "She said friends had turned against you. Seems it had something to do with the fire."

He recognized her pause as invitation to tell her what happened. But his emotions were too raw, his head hurt too much. Opening those wounds would take more effort than he could handle at the moment.

"According to Cora, your experience has taught you both not to trust anyone."

Again, she waited for him to add something. What could he say? He'd learned the cost of trust. He leaned his head against the log wall. "I'm tired."

After a moment, she slipped away. He wondered if she would go home. Instead she joined Cora, and the girls chased the kitten through the trees.

Half his heart ached to let Mandy in. Allow himself to love her.

The other half remembered the price he'd paid because he'd so blindly trusted those he loved. Or supposed he'd loved.

How could he ever take that chance again? Even with a woman like Mandy who risked her life to make sure he was safe.

He shifted so he could watch her play with Cora, making her laugh like a young girl. His eyes ached with longing.

His heart quivered with caution.

Chapter 10

The next morning, he forced his reluctant body to get up and return to work on the house, though at the moment he didn't care whether or not he finished it.

Cora followed him around, keeping a close eye on him.

He stopped to face her. "You can quit worrying. I'm not hurt."

"Trace..." Her pause lasted several beats. "Oh, never mind. There's no use in saying anything." She turned to walk away.

He caught her arm and stopped her. "About what?"

She considered his question and met his gaze. "About everything. About Annabelle and Austin. Mama and Papa. About the fire. And most of all, about you and Mandy."

"Wow, little sister, that's quite a mouthful. Seems you've covered about everything in our lives."

"It is everything in our lives. And it's all gone, destroyed by a stupid fire."

"And the treachery of so-called friends."

Cora pressed Goliath to her cheek. "Will we never again have a normal life?"

Brother and sister studied each other. "Are you saying you want to go to town? Let people see you? That's normal."

Her eyes flooded with tears. "So is letting yourself care about someone."

"I care about you."

"I mean someone outside the family. Like Mandy."

He opened his mouth then closed it. There was nothing to say. He cared for Mandy, but his feelings scared him. Made him feel as if he were the traitor. Turning on his own resolve. He had vowed to never trust another person—man or woman. Apart from Cora, he would live with his heart closed to anything but the most surface of acquaintances. But Mandy with her persistence had forced her way past those barriers.

He resented her doing so.

At the same time—stupid as it was—he ached to open his heart and invite her in.

"I've got work to do." Cora, already mixing up corn bread for lunch, would be okay. He headed for the woods, supposedly to find and cut another tree. In truth, he hoped he could flee his thoughts.

But escape was impossible. He had gone but ten yards when he realized he'd forgotten his ax. He retraced his steps and arrived in the clearing at the same time as Mandy. She saw him and stopped dead still.

His boots refused to take another step. He told his eyes to look for the ax, but they wouldn't leave Mandy's face.

Her expression revealed nothing. Which told him a lot.

That she was guarded after his refusal to talk to her last night. Perhaps wondering if he considered her a friend.

His heart said she was so much more.

But he couldn't admit it. Not because he didn't trust her. She was as guileless as a baby.

He didn't trust his feelings.

Last time he'd trusted in the word *friend* it had cost him everything but his life and Cora's. Last time he trusted a woman, she'd been part of the plan to destroy him.

Confusion knotted his throat, made it impossible to talk, almost impossible to breathe.

Mandy broke the silence. "Morning, Trace. How are you feeling today?"

"Good," he managed to choke out.

"No ill effects from yesterday?"

"Sore throat." It was true, and he hoped she put his hoarseness down to that.

"Mine, too. Joanna made a little honey tonic that calms it. I brought you some." She handed him a flask. "Have sips of it every so often." She pulled a second flask from her pocket and proceeded to take a sip.

He could not force his eyes to leave off watching as she tipped her head back and swallowed.

She capped the flask, returned it to her pocket, and picked up her ax. She noticed he didn't have his and looked around. She spotted it and handed it to him. "Ready to get to work?"

He tried to think what she meant. Finally decided it didn't make any sense. He hoisted his ax to his shoulder. "I was just on my way." He turned and retraced his steps into the woods.

She followed hard on his heels.

He stopped.

She stopped.

He waited for her to pass or head off a different direction, but she didn't. It seemed unusual, but what could he say? She had as much right to walk the ground as did he.

He reached the place where he'd chosen a tree and set to work.

Mandy hovered close by, watching.

He paused. "You taking lessons?" Maybe she wanted to start a proper building. But she didn't stand a chance at catching up.

"Guess you could say I am. I've decided to help you finish your house."

"That knock on my head yesterday must have affected my hearing. Seems like I heard you say you were going to help me."

"You heard right."

It must have affected his reasoning, too. "Why?"

"Because you need it."

"Where do you get that idea?"

"You and Cora need a home. I have one. You want to stay. Seems like a good idea. Besides, seems to me you need to learn that it's possible to have friends and trust them." She measured a tree with her eye. "This looks like a good one. What do you think?"

He'd already picked it out as suitable. "It looks fine."

She set to work.

All he could do was stare. None of what she said made sense. Oh, it made a degree of sense. He needed a house. He had decided to stay here, more out of a need to beat Mandy at her own game than any real conviction that the land was the best in the world. But the rest of it? Total nonsense. "I know how to have friends. Just don't think I need them." He swung his ax at the tree.

"Everyone needs them." She didn't stop swinging her

ax. "Everyone needs people they can trust." Several more swings by each of them. Then she added, "Person just needs to learn which ones are safe."

"Maybe the safest thing is to trust no one."

"Nope." She continued working. "Not safe." *Chop.* "Lonely." *Chop.* "Unnecessary." *Chop.* "Judgmental." *Chop.*

He echoed each of her words with a swing of his own ax. His tree went down first with a ground-shaking thud.

Hers followed two blows later, and she stood back in triumph.

"First real tree you ever felled?"

"Yup." She grinned at him. "Did okay, didn't I?"

"You sure did."

He set about trimming off the limbs. She followed his example. He slowed his pace, afraid she would try and keep up. He didn't want to risk her slipping and cutting herself.

He closed his eyes and sucked in air, stilling the tickle in his raw throat. He didn't know if he could live through another scare with her.

It didn't escape him that a man determined to keep a wide distance between himself and others had a strong reaction to the thought of Mandy being hurt.

"Well, shoot," he muttered. Of course he cared. That wasn't the point. It was all right to care. Just not all right to…well, to rest his heart in the hands of another.

"Something wrong?"

"Nothing. Nothing at all." He bent his attention to his work, aware she watched with avid curiosity. Try as hard as he could, he could not ignore her. He stepped away from the tree to go to her.

She rose, her ax hanging from her hand.

He grabbed her shoulders. "But if I were to trust anyone, it would be you."

There. He'd said it.

The ax slipped from her fingers. She lifted a hand to his cheek. "Why Trace Owens, that's the nicest thing you've ever said to me."

"Don't get too excited."

"Oh no. Heaven forbid." Her eyes shone.

He couldn't think. All he saw was the gentle kindness of her expression, a look reflecting the soul of the woman. He curled his finger and ran it along her jawline. Paused at her chin. Slowly, as if he moved only in his imagination, he tipped her chin upward and caught her mouth with his, lingering a heartbeat, feeling so content nothing else mattered.

She jerked back. "Why did you do that?"

He stepped away, considering her. Unable to read her expression. "Seemed like a good idea at the time." Now he wondered if it was a mistake. He didn't allow his grin to surface. He still wasn't certain about Mandy's reaction. But kissing her was no mistake. He'd learned something. Like how much he cared about this woman.

She planted her fists on her hips. "You shouldn't have done it."

"Why not?"

"A kiss is supposed to mean something."

It did. But he wasn't about to say exactly what. "What's it supposed to mean?"

"I don't know." She grabbed her ax and whacked off a branch. "That there's something special between a man and a woman. Not just a grudging confession that you might trust me." She attacked several more branches. "Might. *Humph*."

He laughed, earning a scalding look.

"And now you mock me?"

"Heaven forbid," he murmured, inordinately pleased by her ire. "But I can't help wondering what the kiss meant to you."

She straightened and glowered at him.

"Well?" he prompted.

She bent her head so he couldn't see her expression. "I don't know."

"Be sure and tell me when you figure it out."

She didn't answer, but a few mutters drifted his way.

He grinned but contained the laughter filling his lungs. She might not take kindly to what she perceived as his enjoyment at her expense. But it felt mighty good to see her at a loss for words.

Mandy's arms ached from the effort she put into swinging the ax—effort driven by frustration. First, Trace reluctantly admitted he might allow himself to trust her. Then he kissed her. On top of that, he had the nerve to laugh. What kind of game was he playing? *I don't think I can trust you as a friend, but I can kiss you?* That was simply wrong to her way of thinking. The trusting and friendship came first. Then the kissing.

At least he hadn't apologized or said he regretted it, or she might have done something *she'd* regret.

Like plant her hands on either side of his face and show him what a kiss really meant.

She chuckled. In fact…

She stalked over to where he worked at wrapping a chain around the log to haul it to the house. "I have something to say to you."

He took his time about straightening, and if she wasn't mistaken, he pushed his shoulders back as if preparing for a showdown. He took even longer turning to face her.

She almost laughed at the way he glanced at her hands to see if she held a weapon of any sort then searched her eyes, trying to guess what she wanted.

She closed the three feet separating them until they stood toe-to-toe. She reached up and planted her palms on his cheeks, felt the roughness of his whiskers, noticed for the first time the way his skin gathered days of sunshine and pocketed them in each pore. She saw the tightening of his mouth as he waited.

No anger remained in her. Not even a smidgen, though she tried to summon the feeling. Her heart beat with a force that made her wonder if it had ever worked at capacity before. A thrill of anticipation skittered up her throat. She didn't know how to contain it. Feared it would take off the top of her head or scorch the soles of her feet. She sucked in air to clear her thoughts. Didn't succeed.

She pulled his face to hers and lifted her lips to his mouth. Felt him start with surprise and then kiss her back.

Oh my. This was supposed to prove something to him. She couldn't remember what. All she knew was this kiss meant something to her besides guarded trust or reluctant friendship.

To Mandy, it meant he'd stolen a place in her heart.

She couldn't say who broke away first, nor if he was as breathless as she, but neither stepped back. Somehow his arms had closed across her back, and hers were pressed to his shoulders.

"You kissed me." He sounded like he'd run a hundred miles through ice and snow, his voice thick and breathy.

"I'll let you try and figure out what it means." Suddenly aware her eyes and expression would likely give away her feelings, she ducked away. "Don't you think it's about time we got these logs to the house and finished the walls? Never know when it might rain. Rainy weather is miserable when you're living in a tent. Far better to be safe and dry in a real house." She knew she rattled out words like some lonesome old woman, but she didn't want to give him a chance to talk about the way she'd kissed him.

"Right. It's time we got a house built."

She wondered at the way he said it, as if they had suddenly become partners. Nor did she want to point out that partners normally trusted each other. She'd decided to help him complete his house, and that's all that mattered.

Yes, she hoped if he stayed around, lived in the house, he might learn to trust people. Trust her. Enough to kiss her for all the right reasons—because he loved her wholly, completely.

They dragged the logs back to the house and notched them. Together they lifted each into place. She tried to think of nothing but the task at hand, but again and again she stole glances at him. What was going through his head? Several times she caught him watching her, and she jerked away. Then she wondered if he was still watching her.

She was glad when it was almost time to return to the stopping house. But when the sun reached the spot midway down the western sky, signaling her need to return, she said, "We can get one more log before I have to go."

"You're sure?"

"I wouldn't say it if I wasn't."

He gave a tight grin, but his eyes smiled more fully. As if he read more into her offer than she wanted him to.

She held his gaze unblinkingly, daring him to say anything. She told herself she only wanted to help complete the house as quickly as possible. In case it rained.

She wondered if she failed to convince him as completely as she failed to convince herself.

The task took longer than she'd anticipated. When they returned to the clearing, she had no choice but to hurry away before Joanna came looking for her. "I've got to get back."

"See you tomorrow," Trace said.

In her imagination his voice rang with a hundred promises of many tomorrows after tomorrow. She was building possibilities in her mind that were more fragile than the twig house.

Trace watched until Mandy was out of sight then sat on the log and contemplated the day. He'd kissed her. He cared about her...a fact he wasn't ready to welcome.

She had kissed him again after spouting off about a kiss meaning something special.

He leaned back, a smile on his lips. She obviously cared about him, or she wouldn't have kissed him.

With a mutter of disgust, he sprang to his feet.

Cora stood close by, leaning over the tree stump that served as a table, scrubbing a baking pan. "Trace, what's wrong?" Her words were shrill with worry.

"Nothing. At least nothing I can do anything about." He wasn't making a lick of sense.

Cora came to his side. "You're upset about something."

He couldn't explain to her when he didn't know himself what bothered him. Was he upset because Mandy cared about him? Or that he cared about her, and the idea scared him?

"Are you thinking about Mama and Papa?"

He wasn't. He'd buried them and moved on. Driven not by sorrow, but by anger.

If he let go of his anger, would his parents' deaths be in vain?

"Cora, I don't even know what I'm thinking. I don't

want our mother and father to be forgotten as if their lives and deaths meant nothing. But—"

"What do you think they would want us to do? How would they want us to live?"

"I don't know. I simply don't know."

"I miss them." Cora sniffed back a sob.

Trace pulled her into his arms and patted her back. "I do, too."

"I'm glad Mama didn't see my scarred face though."

Cora's muffled words against his chest sent a shock through his insides. "Mama wouldn't care. She'd love you just the same."

"I don't know. She used to say I was far prettier than she'd ever been. I think she would be disappointed I no longer am."

Trace pushed her back to look into her eyes then at her burned cheek. He remembered it as fierce red and distorted. When had it started to fade? "Cora, come here." He drew her away from the bench toward the tent, opened the trunk that held his belongings, and pulled out his shaving mirror. "Look at yourself."

She shied away from the mirror and covered her cheek with her hand. "No. I've seen enough of it."

"It's been weeks since you last looked at it." He held the mirror directly before her face.

She closed her eyes.

He shook her gently. "Cora, look at yourself."

She squinted one eye and peeked at the mirror. Drawn perhaps by curiosity, she slowly opened both eyes and peered at her likeness, dropping her hand away from her face. She stared for a long time then looked at Trace. "It's fading."

"Yes, it is." He squatted to face her. "Cora, Mama and Papa would not want you to think you are no longer beautiful. Because you are. I think they would want you to live a full life."

She rocked her head back and forth. "I'm not sure if I can face people."

They studied each other, a great ache consuming Trace's insides. They had lost so much. More than parents. More than a home. More than Cora's unmarred beauty.

They'd lost faith. In people. In life.

Perhaps even in God.

He tried to put his thoughts into words.

Cora nodded as she listened, her expression wavering between miserable agreement and fragile hope. "Do you think the scars inside us will fade in time like my burn?"

"I can't say."

"This Levi, the preacher man, do you suppose he could tell us?"

"Maybe."

"Then you must talk to him."

He chuckled. "Cora, when did you get so decisive? So bossy?"

She nodded her head like their mother did when she'd made a decision and would accept no argument. "Mandy makes me see how strong a woman can be. I want to be like her."

He bolted to his feet. "Heaven forbid."

But as he strode over to the house, intent on escape, Cora's laughter followed.

His little sister was growing up. Perhaps the lessons she absorbed from watching Mandy would serve her well, make her grow strong.

He grinned. Mandy was strong, independent.

His smile flattened. She was also an idealist—especially when it came to matters of the heart. From what she and her sisters said, she hankered for a father who often left them on their own. He turned to stare at her twig house. Why would she be willing to give up her goal of persuading her pa to settle down here?

Or had she?

Hadn't he learned what happens when people must choose between two loyalties? Friendship held a flickering candle to the strong light of family and obligations.

Where did that leave Trace?

He straightened his shoulders. He'd given his heart to a woman, trusted her, and she'd used his weakness to draw him away from his home. His absence made it possible for the Bushwhackers' attack. How could he ever trust again?

Chapter 11

Trace's self-constructed inner path grew more and more narrow by the day as Mandy worked at his side, ever cheerful, usually teasing, often amusing, and sometimes downright confrontational.

The house was about ready for a roof.

Would she stop visiting once it was finished?

The idea brought on a feeling of emptiness.

Mandy stood back, admiring the structure they had worked so hard to build. "It will be a fine house."

"Good enough for Cora and me." Why did his mind picture someone other than Cora sharing the rooms? Someone like Mandy?

"Tomorrow is Sunday," she said.

"So it is. A day of rest."

"And worship." She turned to give him a serious look that unsettled every effort he'd made to push her away.

"Trace, why don't you come to church with me? You and Cora?"

Cora, listening nearby, said, "I told him he should go and talk to the preacher man."

Mandy grinned. "There you go. Cora has a reason for you to talk to Levi."

He didn't bother to correct her. "I don't have to go to church to talk to Levi, do I?"

"Wouldn't hurt you none."

He laughed. "You calling me a sinner?" He didn't need her accusation to know he was—and the worst sort. Hadn't Jesus said if he didn't forgive, he couldn't be forgiven? Or something like that? He couldn't recall the exact words.

She grinned without apology. "We're all sinners. That's why Jesus came. That's why we need to gather together and be reminded how to deal with the problem."

Cora joined them and nudged Trace. "Go. Mama and Papa would want you to."

He frowned at her. "Cora, you are spending too much time with Mandy and learning some of her underhanded tricks."

"Me?" Mandy sputtered. "Underhanded tricks? You take that back."

He didn't know what she intended to do to him for his remark, but he didn't plan to hang around to find out. He raced for the woods. She'd have to catch him to exact payment, and he didn't intend to let her.

"Cora, help me catch him," Mandy called, already hot on his heels. Then silence. Did he hear whispering? He edged around a tree to see what they were up to.

Mandy had her back to him, but the way their heads bent together, it was obvious the two of them planned something. Something that involved catching him.

Not if he could help it.

He slipped away, silent as a shadow, circling higher and then cutting down the hill to backtrack. He passed beneath them. Cora's passage was unmistakable, the way she crunched over the pine needles. She was no hunter. He had to concentrate to hear Mandy, but after a moment he did. Both of them still followed his path.

He wondered if Mandy would be good enough to pick up his back trail.

A few minutes later he returned to the clearing and moved to the far edge, where he hunkered out of sight behind some bushes. He made himself comfortable. After all, he might be there some time.

He leaned his head back against the trunk of a tree, his thoughts racing. Go to church? His anger and the resulting guilt would surely make him uncomfortable, but all this talk with Cora about what their parents would want had him reconsidering some of his decisions. They would expect their offspring to attend church. Even more, to live Christian lives. He might force himself to go. But he wouldn't force Cora.

He sensed someone watching him. Not moving, careful not to give away any indication of his notice, he scoured the surrounding area thoroughly. Had to stifle a laugh of amusement as he made out Mandy pressed to a tree trunk, invisible to a more casual observer.

He wasn't surprised she'd found him without giving away her approach. In fact, he expected it. But he intended to let her make the first move.

He tipped his head back, lowered his hat to shade his eyes, and pretended to sleep. All the while he watched her, saw how she studied him as if she wanted something from him. Or to give him something.

Her posture relaxed. She knew he'd seen her.

"Okay, I'll go to church with you," he said.

"Great. Cora," she yelled, "he's over here."

Cora tripped through the woods, not at all concerned about how much racket she made.

"He said he'd go to church. You're coming, aren't you?"

Cora stopped still. She shot a look toward Trace so full of longing and aching it brought him to his feet. "Cora, come with me."

Then she closed up like a locked door. "I couldn't."

How he hurt for the pain and isolation his younger sister endured.

Mandy slipped to his side. "One day she will realize people will care about her if she gives them a chance. In the meantime, I mean to be her friend."

Trace reached for Mandy's hand and squeezed it, welcoming her steadfastness.

Cora looked at their joined hands and grinned.

Trace couldn't say who pulled away first, but he and Mandy sprang apart with a sudden need to return to the clearing.

Sunday dawned clear and sunny—perfect for an outdoor service. Mandy had wondered more than once if Trace would truly come. But now she sat on the grassy slope with Trace at her side, waiting for the service to begin. He wore an especially fine white shirt and black trousers she'd never seen before. With a start, she wondered if he'd worn them to his parents' funeral. She shifted her hand, intending to squeeze his and offer silent comfort. But they sat in plain view of a whole bunch of people, and even though they were outdoors, this was church.

Besides, what was she thinking? It seemed ever since

she'd kissed him, her heart did strange things. Like give her this sudden urge to comfort him. Or the inner demand he attend church with her. So many other things, too, like dreaming about him at night. Often in her dreams they were sitting side by side under the stars, his arm around her, holding her close. She would tip her face to him, and he would kiss her. A couple of times, Glory had kicked her awake. Demanded to know why she laughed in her sleep.

It would take four Glorys and half a dozen strong men to pull the truth from her. Likely even then she wouldn't confess.

Any more than she'd admit how longingly she looked at the almost-finished house and imagined cooking over a stove, sitting before the fire with Trace and reading to each other.

At last Levi stood, drawing her away from thoughts of sharing her life with Trace.

Levi welcomed everyone, opened in prayer, then announced a hymn. There were no hymn books, so they sang from memory. And no musical instruments. But Mandy enjoyed hearing the voices next to her. Mr. Phelps had a deep voice like a bullfrog. Joanna sang clear as a bell. Levi carried them all along with his strong voice. And Trace...

Mandy decided he must have the voice of an angel—a man angel, if there were such things. A solid, pleasantly mellow voice. She had to force her attention to remain on Levi while her errant, willful heart longed to look at Trace, meet his eyes, and join her voice to his as if there were no others present.

The hymn ended, and her heart knocked at her ribs. Such a demanding part of her body. She hadn't noticed it till lately.

They sang three more hymns, Mandy's enjoyment growing with each verse. Then Levi opened his Bible.

"Today I am reading from Matthew chapter five, verses one to twelve, what we commonly call the Beatitudes."

Mandy leaned forward as he spoke on the blessings of doing things God's way.

Could she possibly expect to be blessed when she constantly insisted on doing things her way? When she chafed at God for allowing Pa to abandon them?

The service ended. Many recognized Trace from last Sunday and crossed to his side to speak to him and thank him for rescuing the Murrays.

"How are they?" he asked one man.

"Fine. Temporarily living in the back of the office while they rebuild. Mrs. Murray says now she can have a house with a little more style."

Mandy stayed close to him, proud to be his friend. Even if he wanted to hide Cora, there was no need for Trace to secrete himself away from others.

He joined them again for dinner.

"Mandy made the dessert," Glory announced as if she'd done it 'specially for Trace.

"It's only a chocolate cake pudding." She tried to find Glory's ankle under the table, but Glory stayed out of the way and grinned with a great deal of triumph.

Trace tasted it. "Fantastic."

Levi echoed his comment. "Maybe you could teach Glory to make it." Which earned him an elbow to his ribs.

Unrepentant, he laughed.

Trace let out a deep-throated chuckle, and Mandy angled her body toward him. She quirked an eyebrow.

His eyes shone like summer sunshine. "I find you Buffalo Gals amusing"—he must have read her warning not to mock them—"in a purely delightful way." He shifted his gaze to encompass the other sisters. "You're all as strong as any woman I've ever met, and many a man. You're adventuresome, hardworking, and not afraid of risks. Quite unlike the young women I knew back in Missouri. I admire you." His eyes made their way back to Mandy and probed deep into her thoughts.

It felt as if the words were meant for her alone.

"Thank you," Joanna and Glory said. "We try our best," Glory added.

"I couldn't agree more," Levi added. "Though you forgot one important characteristic."

Trace turned toward Levi, and Mandy turned her attention to him, too, with some reluctance.

"Yup," Levi said. "You forgot wild and rebellious." Which earned him another jab of Glory's sharp elbow and a chuckle from Trace.

Mandy and Glory studied each other, plotting revenge.

"Oh, oh," Levi said. "I'm going to pay for that."

"Unless you can outrun them." Trace's voice rang with amusement.

"I'm not even going to try." He leaned toward Glory and kissed her on the nose. "I don't want to miss the fun."

It didn't take a genius to see Glory had forgotten any thoughts of payback.

Mandy couldn't drum up much interest either.

They finished the meal and worked together to clean up the kitchen. Both Trace and Levi offered to help with supper preparations; then they all escaped to the sun-filled yard.

"We're going to check on the folks at the mission." Although the building wasn't finished, Levi had taken in an injured man and his very pregnant wife. "Anyone want to come along?" Levi asked.

Joanna shook her head. "I have a few things I want to do on my own." She emphasized the last two words as if indicating she would be relieved to be free of them all.

Mandy studied her eldest sister as tendrils of worry and fear threaded through her heart. "Are you getting tired of us hanging about?"

"Mandy, I didn't mean anything except I don't mind being here on my own. Now off you go, and enjoy the afternoon." She waved them away.

Trace said he wouldn't mind seeing the mission. Mandy remembered Cora wanted him to talk to Levi about something. But she wanted to show Trace some of the special spots around Bonners Ferry. "We'll be along in a bit."

Glory planted herself in front of Mandy, ready to tease her.

But before she could spit the words out, Levi grabbed her hand. "Come on, Glory." Glory jerked back, unwilling to give up her plan so quickly.

"Let it go," Levi said.

Glory squinted at Mandy then allowed Levi to lead her away.

Finally Trace and Mandy were alone except for those going about their business, unmindful of the pair. And Mandy couldn't decide where to look. Certainly not at him. What if he saw the burst of joy blaze across her face?

"Come on," she murmured, hurrying in the general direction of the ferry.

"Aren't we going with Levi and Glory?"

"In a roundabout way. I want to show you something first. Is that okay?" She finally turned, finally met his gaze. Almost wished she hadn't. But not quite. She could swim in the blue of his eyes, drown in the fondness she saw…or let herself think she saw.

They walked side by side past the scattered buildings at this end of town. She led him up a rocky path until they met up with the narrow stream and stopped at its bank. The water chattered noisily across rocks. She wanted to say something about how she found the noise of the water both cheering and calming. But she couldn't find the words. So she let him look and listen without comment.

"The sound of running water is hypnotizing." His voice was all soft and mellow.

"I like it."

"Me, too." He reached for her hand. "Me, too."

She wasn't certain if he still referred to the running water. And didn't care. Being here, sharing her love of nature, feeling at peace with herself and this man—it was all that mattered at the moment.

"Let's keep climbing." She indicated the path by the stream, and they moved upward, their feet padding softly on the leafy ground, the sun warming them despite the canopy of trees crowding toward the stream. In many places the passage was too narrow to walk side by side, and he led the way. As soon as the path widened, he waited for her and again took her hand.

Mandy discovered something satisfying, and at the same time frightening, about the clasp of her hand in his. It made her want things she thought only Pa could give—home, belonging, and so much more.

In a short time they reached a wider spot where the water had spread into a pool. "This is my favorite place." She led him to a fallen tree where she often sat to watch the animals tiptoe in for water. "I've seen so many animals. I never shoot anything here. Seems the animals deserve to know this place is theirs."

They sat side by side, the quiet sifting into her thoughts,

her soul. She wondered if he felt the same blessed peace. Her hand lay in his.

He shifted. "Mandy, what did you think of the sermon?"

She gathered her impressions into some sort of order. "I know I should trust God more. Like when I get upset and sad because I miss Pa. I wonder why God doesn't stop him and make him come back and live with us."

Trace threaded his fingers between hers and curled his over the top, protectively—or so she let herself think. "I suppose it's because God doesn't force us to do anything."

"But He could stop Pa, couldn't He?"

"He has the power to do so, of course. But not the will."

She understood, but… "Sometimes it's hard to trust God."

He examined each of her fingers then stared at the shadowed water. "Blessed are the merciful, for they shall be shown mercy."

"That's one of the Beatitudes Levi read, isn't it?"

She felt Trace's tension. Knew something about the words bothered him.

"I don't know if I can show mercy."

"To whom?"

"I told you my parents died in a fire." His voice seemed heavy with sorrow.

"Yes." She had nothing to offer by way of comfort but her quiet presence.

"What I didn't tell you was the fire was deliberately set."

She gasped. "They were murdered?" A shudder raced through her. "That's terrible."

He gripped her hand so hard her fingers hurt, but she

didn't pull away. "My best friend was one of those who did it."

She could feel his pain like sharp needles all over her body. "That's why you don't trust people."

He nodded. His shoulders slumped forward the way Cora's often did.

"Trace, I'm so sorry." She rubbed his back, trying to soothe him like Joanna did for her. "Why would your friend do that?"

"Because he wasn't really a friend." Bitterness edged each word.

"I'm sorry." The words were inadequate, but she had no others to offer.

"Just because my father was a hero in the Mexican-American War."

Mandy didn't see how that constituted a reason, but it seemed to make sense for Trace.

"Everyone assumed he was Unionist because of that. He did his best to stay out of the Civil War. Said he'd seen enough fighting to last ten lifetimes. Said problems should be dealt with by negotiations, not by killing each other."

The pain pouring out with each word scraped at the inside of Mandy's heart until she wondered it wasn't in shreds.

"My friend"—he made the term sound positively hateful—"joined the Bushwhackers for the Confederates. As if it made running with a bunch of lawless renegades somehow more legitimate. They loot, burn, and take advantage of defenseless women. They honor no law, nor any person's rights apart from their own." He spit out each word like the pit from a sour fruit.

She continued to rub his back, though she ached to do so much more. Pull him into her arms and hold him tight. But no amount of comfort she offered would erase the pain from his soul.

Only time and God's love could do that. Not something she'd given a lot of thought to until this moment. But seeing Trace's misery, knowing how it felt to be mortally disappointed by others whether a close friend or a pa, she knew healing lay outside human resources.

"I knew a girl back then. Annabelle Jones. I thought she had some regard for me. But it was all pretend. Austin—the man I thought was my friend—got Annabelle to lure me away from our house. While I was gone, they set it afire. My mother and father were resting and died on their bed."

His body shuddered.

Mandy pressed her cheek to his shoulder. "Cora?" she whispered.

"I heard people rushing to fight the fire. Didn't even consider it might be my own home. Annabelle tried to hold me back. 'It's too late,' she said. But I wouldn't be stopped. Even when men tried to prevent me from going in, I pushed them aside. I found Cora trying to get to the door and pulled her to safety. She was burned. But you know that. Oh, Mandy. It was awful. How will I ever forget?" He faced her, his eyes brimming with sorrow.

Although her heart gathered up his pain until every pulse hurt, she did not shrink from meeting his gaze. She hoped he could read her unspoken thoughts of comfort and caring.

He wrapped an arm around her shoulder and with a muffled groan pulled her to his chest. "Mandy." That was all he said, her name a sound of despair.

She edged her arms around him and held him close. Sharing his sorrow as best she could.

152   *Mandy and the Missouri Man*

He shuddered again then his breathing evened out. "Mandy." This time her name carried something more.

She couldn't let herself think what.

His arms tightened. "I cannot forgive them. I cannot show mercy."

What she heard was not unforgiveness but lostness. She had no words for him on either subject, but she recognized them as her own. She often felt that sense of lostness about her pa. Only she'd never truly recognized it. Needing guidance, she offered up a tentative prayer. *God, I don't often come to You for anything, but Trace needs Your help today.* She should try and get him to walk with her toward the mission. Levi could help him.

But he showed no sign of releasing her, and she didn't intend to free herself.

"I wish I could forget the whole thing. My so-called friends, the way the community turned a blind eye to the fact two murders had been committed…everything. But I can't."

She offered up another silent prayer. Trace must find a way to forgive those dreadful people, or his own soul would suffer. "The trouble with bitterness is it hurts the man who carries it. Not the person to whom it is directed. It's like drinking poison."

"I'm learning that. But I don't see any way out of it."

She edged back to look into his face. "What if this Austin fellow repented of what he'd done? Could you forgive him then?"

He searched her gaze. "I simply don't know."

"What if"—she could barely bring the name to her lips—"Annabelle came to you and said she was sorry?"

She felt his careful consideration of her question. Would he decide to return and explore this possibility? If he did, she could have the house. Not even a flicker of joy accompanied the thought, because she didn't want it. She wanted Trace. Wanted him to stay here. Live here.

"I think I can forget Annabelle's part in this treachery. She is a silly girl who doesn't know what she wants. Likely she'll marry someone who appreciates her charm and simplicity."

Mandy's heart lifted with relief.

"But Austin and I grew up together. I always thought we would stand shoulder to shoulder in any challenge and fight side by side to the end."

Mandy tried to imagine how she'd feel if Glory or Joanna had betrayed her. Couldn't picture it. But even the thought made her insides feel like they'd been melted and poured out.

"How do I forgive and forget?"

"I don't have the answers. Maybe Levi does."

But neither of them made a move toward resuming their journey. Instead, they shifted to contemplate the pond and their thoughts. Trace's arm remained across her shoulders, and she clutched his other hand.

"It's peaceful here," Trace said after a bit. "The troubles of the world seem far away."

"That's why it's my favorite spot."

He caught her chin and tipped her face toward him. "What troubles do you have, Mandy?"

She hesitated, deciding to trust him just as he had trusted her. "I struggle with forgiveness, too. It's nothing like what you have to deal with, but I'm often angry with Pa for leaving us." She wondered if he heard the quiver in her voice. "It's something I only recently realized. I always believed what Glory said…. I was trying to make him into an ideal parent. But it's far more than that." She sat up and faced him, finding courage in the steady way he regarded her. "I'm angry at him."

Trace nodded. "Sometimes it's hard to forgive."

"But not impossible."

"How is it possible? Tell me. I want to know."

How could she explain when she didn't understand it herself? "I think it has something to do with allowing a different feeling to control me."

"Like what?"

Like my growing feelings for you. Trace, I think I love you. But she couldn't say the words. Feared that doing so would put a vast gulf between them. "Maybe being in competition with you over building our houses made it possible to forget my anger. It lost its hold on me." She concentrated on the trees beyond his ear, unwilling to meet his gaze directly, lest he guess the truth.

He chuckled. "I, too, forgot to be angry while you were around building your twig house."

She laughed along with him, wondering what he felt about her.

A duck quacked across the pond, her gaggle of ducklings paddling after her.

With a sigh of regret, Mandy realized how long they'd lingered. "Glory will come looking for us any minute."

"Let's be on our way." He reached for her hand and pulled her to her feet.

Hand in hand, they walked back to the roadway and within minutes reached the mission.

Mandy hadn't been to visit in some time, and the amount of work accomplished stunned her. The main building was almost finished. "You two have been busy."

"We've had lots of help," Levi said. "It will soon be ready. I can hardly wait."

But the way his eyes rested on Glory, bringing a pink blush to her cheeks, Mandy knew his impatience was more about wanting to marry than wanting to open the mission.

She didn't envy her sister's happiness, but would she ever know the same? She didn't dare look at Trace nor any of the others for fear they could read her longing.

Chapter 12

Trace accompanied Levi on a tour of the frame construction. Large enough to house a number of people in need of care, with living quarters for Levi and Glory as well. Trace heard the explanation with half his attention.

Something had happened between himself and Mandy as he confessed his feelings about the incident that took his parents' lives. Something warm and wonderful and full of promises for the future. But had she felt it, too?

He almost hoped she hadn't, because until he could get rid of his bitterness toward Austin and the others—a bitterness that boiled over toward God—he could not offer her unfettered love.

They left the building and walked across the yard until they came to a corral of horses.

"These are the animals Glory works with, healing abused and neglected horses."

"Does a horse always recover from such things?"

"With enough kindness. Glory is willing to give what it takes."

"Can people recover from similar misfortunes or treachery or…" He didn't know what he wanted to ask.

Levi faced him. "Are we talking about something specific, or just general conversation?"

"Do you have time to listen to my tale of woe?"

"Always." They leaned against the top board of the fence as Trace retold his story.

"Can a man forgive such things?" Trace gripped the railing, hoping for an answer but unable to see a way. "Can I trust a God who allowed it? Can I ever love again after experiencing such betrayal at the hands of people I considered friends?"

"The short answer is yes. But I think you know that. What you really want to know is how."

"Exactly."

Levi took a deep breath, watching a gray mare canter around the fence. "Again, the short answer is by trusting God. But that's too simplistic. Perhaps I should tell you my own experience. My brother and I were orphaned as youngsters and went to live with my grandparents, who were very strict. My brother refused to adjust. He threw their rules over his shoulder and left. But he wasn't content with walking away from their rules. He also ignored man-made rules and God's rules and ended up in prison, where he is even now."

"I'm sorry to hear that. It must be hard."

"It is." Levi turned to Trace, studying him. "But my reaction was to bargain with God. Tell Him if I served him as a preacher, then He was obligated to turn Matt around. I made a vow that almost cost me a chance for life with Glory. In hindsight, I can't imagine how I could have even thought God wanted me to do such a thing."

Trace wondered what this story had to do with him.

"My whole point is this—God is not responsible for the choices people make, but He is faithful to what He has promised."

Trace tried to think of a promise to cover the betrayal of friends, the murder of his parents, and the anger in his heart. He shook his head.

"I don't have any cure-all answer for you." Levi stared into the distance. "But remember Jesus was betrayed, murdered, and yet allowed it so He could provide salvation for us all. 'With God all things are possible.' Even impossible things like forgiveness."

Trace's jaw clenched. "My friends are responsible for murder."

"I agree. But justice will prevail. If not in this life then in the next."

"That hardly seems like justice."

"God is never early and never late."

Glory called out an invitation for refreshments, and the conversation ended. They joined the sisters and visited over tea and cake.

Mandy glanced at the position of the sun. "We need to get back and help Joanna."

"And I need to get back to Cora," Trace said. He and Mandy headed down the trail, leaving Glory to say her good-byes.

Mandy barely waited until they were out of earshot to speak. "Did Levi say anything helpful?"

He wished he could assure her that, thanks to Levi, all his problems were gone, but he couldn't. "He said, 'With God all things are possible.' I haven't figured out how that helps me. I guess it doesn't."

"But maybe it will. Seems it's impossible for us to forgive some things. Maybe only God can forgive."

"But who is He to forgive—Austin, for his treachery, or me for not forgiving Austin?"

Mandy stopped in front of him, preventing him from continuing. She faced him. "Why not both?"

"Austin doesn't deserve forgiveness."

"True. But if he repented?"

"Mandy, it makes me angry to think he can just say sorry and be done with it. That's not fair."

"I suppose not." She studied the sky for a moment as if seeking answers from above. "But when you think about it, all of us are undeserving of God's forgiveness." Her gaze returned to his, warm and gentle. "We don't deserve His love, but He gives it anyway."

He couldn't resist the look of peace on her face and cupped his hand to the back of her head. "Mandy, if I were free to love…" Why go on when he wasn't?

"Why aren't you? You still in love with Annabelle?"

"No." He scowled. "I never loved her."

"Then what's keeping you from loving?"

Did she have any idea how appealing she looked as she probed his heart? Was she suggesting she loved him?

"Mandy, how can I love freely when my heart is consumed by bitterness? Hate? Hate has the power to poison love. I don't think there is room for both. Until I can deal with it, I cannot offer my love." He should break away, put distance between them, but she clamped her hands to his shoulders and smiled so sweetly and gently his heart threatened to melt. "When I sort this out…" His throat had grown so tight his words came out husky. He could speak no promises, but he could let her get a glimpse of the love in his heart.

He bent and kissed her, breathing in her wildflower scent until he could barely think. But he must think. He must be rational. Until there was nothing in his heart competing with his love for her. He slowly lifted his head.

Her eyes were dark pools of emotion. She opened her mouth, and he feared she would demand he speak the words his kiss hinted at. He could not. Before she could say anything, he took her hand and continued down the trail.

Mandy knew Trace's kiss was a silent promise of love. But he feared what lay in his heart. Who could blame him for his bitterness? Why did such awful things happen?

As Levi often said, it was easy to blame God for what man was responsible for. She could do nothing more than pray for Trace to find healing. And continue to show her love for him.

But he sure knew how to make it difficult.

The next morning she raced through her chores at the stopping house and hurried up the trail.

Perhaps by now he'd sorted out his feelings and was ready to move on.

She stepped into the clearing and halted. Cora huddled by the fire, sobbing. Trace knelt beside her.

Mandy rushed to them. "What's wrong?" She squatted beside Cora and rubbed her back. "Cora, what happened?"

Cora sobbed harder, unable to speak.

Mandy hadn't allowed herself to look directly at Trace yet and steeled herself to meet his gaze. She'd hoped for signs of love but saw only raw anger. She asked her question again, directing it this time at Trace.

He sprang to his feet, shoved his hand through his hair, strode three feet away, then turned. "Some young fella saw the smoke from our campfire and thought he'd pay a neighborly visit. No one invited him, but I suppose it's a free country." He reeled about and walked the same three feet, spun around, and stomped back to his original spot. "He saunters in here all friendly. Asks if he can join us for breakfast. I tried to shoo him off, but he saw Cora at the fire and wouldn't pay any heed to me."

Cora sobbed harder.

"Cora had left her bonnet off. She couldn't get it before the young buck sauntered up to her, bold as brass, and said he'd like to make her acquaintance. I grabbed a branch, prepared to persuade him to leave us alone. But then he saw her face and changed his mind so fast he almost tripped over his feet getting out of here."

Trace kicked dirt into the fire until it was buried.

Mandy pulled Cora into her arms and patted her back. But a suspicion grew in her mind. "Is this where you were sitting?"

Cora nodded.

"Trace, is that the branch you picked up?" She pointed to one a few feet past Cora.

"I should have applied it to his backside."

"Did the young man come from up the trail or down the trail?"

"I suppose down. He stepped into the clearing over there and made his way to the fire." Trace pointed.

"Oh, honestly, Trace." A bubble of amusement rose to the back of her throat, but she feared her laughter would offend Cora. "Did you ever consider it wasn't Cora's scars he saw but a big, angry man with a fat stick in his hands?"

Trace scowled.

But Cora sat up, wiped her eyes, and sniffled into a hankie. She looked from the branch to the place where the man had stood. She glared at Trace, his face twisted in anger. "You scared him off, you big oaf." She started to laugh.

Mandy could no longer contain her amusement.

Trace frowned at the pair of them, laughing hard enough to bring on tears. He stalked into the woods without a backward look.

Mandy scrambled to her feet and followed.

She found him deep in the woods, slamming his fist into a tree. She choked back a scream. Why was he throwing a temper tantrum? She stepped forward and grabbed his arm before he could hit the tree again. His knuckles were bloodied. Her own anger flared. "What is this accomplishing?"

He jerked his arm free and turned his back to her. His neck muscles corded. His shoulders pulled forward.

"Trace, it was a mistake. Anyone would have fled when they saw you approaching. I doubt it had anything to do with Cora's cheek."

"You can't say that with any certainty."

She glared at him. "Just as you can't say with any certainty it was Cora's scars that scared him away." She crossed her arms, waiting for his anger to abate, but he remained as rigid as any of the logs he'd cut for the house.

"This is what I mean about hate poisoning everything. Including me. I am so angry I am on fire inside." The words ground out so hard she wouldn't have been surprised to see bits of tooth enamel accompany them. "I know it can consume me." He strode away, resting one hand on a nearby tree, blood oozing from his knuckles. He let his head fall forward. "Until I find a way to erase it…"

She heard what he didn't say. Until that time, he would not allow himself to love. And yet… She forced some patience into her voice and repeated an idea she'd expressed yesterday. "Perhaps the way to get rid of hate is to replace it with something." She waited, but he gave no indication if he heard or understood her meaning. Pain or no pain, she had absolutely no sympathy for letting events control him. Enough was enough. "Look if you want to spend your life wallowing in your hurts, fine. But did it ever occur to you that maybe letting love into your heart can rid it of hate and anger?" She moved to his side and touched his arm, felt him twist beneath her palm. "Trace?" Was he ready to quit being an idiot?

He faced her, his eyes dark as still, deep water, his mouth drawn back into a thin line of despair. "Don't you see," he whispered. "I love you, but love hasn't erased my hate."

"You love me?" Did she sound as surprised and happy as she felt? Annoyed, too. This was not the moment he should have confessed his love.

"Forget I said it. I can't love you, can't offer you what you deserve until I do something about this." He slammed his bloodied fist into his chest. "I don't recognize myself when I'm like this. I don't trust myself."

Unbelievable. Part of her ached to tend his wounds—hold him close and assure him he was fine just the way he was. But she sensed he was as angry at himself and his inability to handle his emotions as he was about his past. She wondered if anything she said at this point would make a difference. Likely not. Besides another part of her wanted to shake him hard and tell him to look at what the future held for those ready and willing to forget the past. But what was the use? She shook her head. "Let's go work on the house." She headed toward the clearing.

With a heavy sigh, he followed.

They soon settled into a soothing rhythm of work.

Cora, Goliath in her arms, sauntered over to watch. "What are you going to do with Mandy's house?"

"You mean the twig house?" Trace teased.

Relieved to see his normal good humor restored, Mandy pretended to get all defensive. "No wolf is going to blow it down. It will suit just fine for an outbuilding."

"I don't know." Trace circled her little shack, touched each corner, and each time jumped back as if afraid it would come crashing down.

"Let's see how hard you can blow," she challenged.

His eyes crinkled at the corners in a hidden smile; then he blew and blew until he had to bend over his knees to get his breath.

"See, I told you."

"I doubt if my little puffs will be the worst thing this shack has to endure. What about the winds, the rain, the snow?"

She went to his side and contemplated the building. Wasn't much to look at, but she wasn't going to confess it to him. "It'll stand the winter."

"Maybe. Then crumble into the soil."

"Dying a natural death as all things do." She cocked her head at Trace and added, "All things pass…even emotions. If we give them half a chance."

He lifted his eyebrows skyward as he understood her message. "But this has the elements to wear it down."

"And you have God's love and forgiveness to wear down your hate."

"Hasn't helped much so far." He wheeled around and bent over a log, notching it.

Day after day they worked on the house. The roof would soon be finished. It was satisfying to see progress.

But despite Mandy's reassurance that his emotions would change, Trace saw no progress in conquering his hate and lack of forgiveness. Every time he looked at Cora, he remembered Austin and the others. Even building this log cabin was a reminder. They'd once had a fine, big house.

Cora wandered around the interior of the cabin, which didn't take more than a few steps. "Where will you put the stove?" she called.

He'd shown her before but went inside. "The stove will go here, so it can warm the whole room. The area closest to the door will be the kitchen and living area. The bedrooms will be on this side. I'll build partitions so we can have privacy."

"What will we do for furnishings?"

"I can make a table and some chairs. Maybe even a rocking chair."

"I wish we had some of Mama's quilts for the bed."

Mandy joined them.

It no longer surprised him to have her appear suddenly and silently.

"I saw some nice fabric at the store," she said. "You could make one for your bed."

Cora's eyes brightened. "That might be fun."

Every nerve in Trace's body fired up with awareness of Mandy in the confines of the cabin. His mind flooded with imaginations. Not for the first time, he thought of her residing here. Sitting in a rocking chair mending something.

He snorted. More likely she'd be out hunting. He tried to dispel the longing that clutched his throat. Because he knew she could cook if she wanted to. He'd seen her mend a tear in her pants with neat tight stitches that even his mother would have praised.

Cora took his sound of disbelief for criticism. "You don't think I can make a quilt?"

"I'm quite certain you can." He wondered how hard to push her. "Question is, will you go to town and select the fabric you like or ask Mandy to do it and settle for what she picks out?"

Mandy's mouth flew open. She stared at him but remained silent.

Cora opened her mouth. Then she touched her cheek and turned away. "I expect we have enough bedding to do us."

Mandy lifted one shoulder in a little shrug.

Trace strode from the house. What right did he have to try and change Cora? He couldn't even change himself.

Mandy followed. "One day she will decide to go to town. She might learn no one cares about her burn half as much as she does. And you." She stalked away before he could point out a differing opinion. In truth, he couldn't find one. Understood the scar on Cora's face was no more disfiguring or difficult to ignore than the hate weighing his heart.

Something landed on his neck. He brushed it away. It happened again. He rubbed at the spot, caught something in his finger, and pulled his hand forward to see a small piece of wood. Like one he'd chopped from a log.

Another hit his neck and then his shoulder. Several hit his head.

If he wasn't mistaken, he heard muffled laughter from around the corner of the cabin.

So Mandy wanted to play, did she?

He brushed at his neck again and complained about the bugs. Then pretended to head toward the tent for something. As soon as he knew he was out of her sight, he changed direction and edged around the walls. He paused at the last corner, listening to her quiet breathing as she listened for him.

He gathered air into his lungs and eased around the corner.

She had her back to him, leaning forward, trying to see where he'd gone.

He tiptoed toward her. When she stiffened, caught some indication of him behind her, he sprang forward and captured her.

She squealed and struggled, but he wouldn't let her escape. She squirmed until she faced him.

"Think it's funny to play tricks on me, do you?" he asked.

A smile wreathed her face and flashed through her eyes as she nodded. Her smile softened as she gave a look so full of promise and longing he thought his heart would burst from his chest. Loving this woman would be such sweet joy. Every day would be full of fun and warmth.

As they considered each other, letting their gazes linger, the air shimmered with hope and possibility.

"Where did you guys go?" Cora called from inside the cabin.

The reality of his life erased the glow of the moment. He let his arms fall to his sides and stepped back. "We're out here."

Mandy reached for him.

He shook his head. "Don't. I can't."

Her hand hung suspended between them, and her face filled with sorrow.

He hated that he was responsible. But he'd tried to replace his hatred with love. But hate poisoned everything.

With a grumble, he ground around and headed for the woods.

How was he to deal with this?

The answers were easy. Forgive and let God exact justice. Trust God's ways. God's ways were higher than man's ways.

But knowing the answers and being able to do them weren't the same thing.

He made no attempt to slip through the woods quietly but crashed past trees, glad of the noise he made, finding relief in bending branches out of his way and hearing them snap back.

He didn't know how long he tromped on in that fashion, but he reached the side of a hill and looked out over the wide valley. The view reminded him of the one he'd seen soon after he'd met Mandy and how he'd called her to share it.

The beauty sucked at his insides.

"Oh God," he yelled, "show me how to forgive." But the words fell into the distance like pebbles dropped in a bottomless pit. Like every desperate prayer he'd uttered over the past days.

Would he never find a way to get rid of the curse of hatred? Would he be forever trapped in this pit? Never able to give his heart in complete, unfettered love to the woman he cared for?

Chapter 13

A dozen days later, Mandy helped Joanna serve the evening meal. Glory was absent, helping Levi with something. Twenty men clustered around the table, eagerly scooping up generous helpings. Talk, as usual, consisted mostly of questions about the gold fields to the north.

Joanna answered as best she could. Mandy said little, her thoughts still back up the hill with Trace and Cora.

She loved Trace and knew he loved her. He'd said so, but then said love wasn't possible.

But she wouldn't entertain the word *impossible*. If he couldn't make up his own mind, she'd make it up for him.

In the intervening days she'd prayed as never before. Borrowed Mother's Bible from Joanna and read it, searching for answers. She'd found none that might help Trace, but something had been happening in her own soul. Hope and assurance of God's love filled her, replacing her anger at Pa. She felt blessed. She wanted Trace to find the same thing.

Every day she told him of verses she'd read or how she felt. He always grew hopeful. Hunger filled his eyes. Then he glanced away, often toward the house, or Cora, and she knew the memories had come flooding back. He could not let go of his bitterness.

She could only take a deep breath, swallow her frustration, and continue to pray and love him, hoping at some point both would heal his spirit.

Something in the conversation around the table caught her attention, and she looked at the man who'd spoken. "Who did you say you are looking for?"

"Trace Owens."

That's what she thought. "What's your business with him?"

"It's of a personal nature, but it's imperative I contact him."

"And who might you be?"

Most of the others excused themselves and went outdoors, having no interest in a conversation that didn't have the word *gold* in it. Joanna let Mandy do the talking, but her interest was also focused on this stranger who asked after Trace.

"My name is Austin Collins."

Austin! The man who'd betrayed Trace...caused his parents' deaths and Cora's scars. She studied the man. As blond as Trace. As big. And every bit as sad and bitter looking. The way his mouth sagged, she wondered if he had any smile muscles in his face.

Two unhappy men. But she would not tell him where Trace was. Surely it would destroy Trace's very soul to be faced with the man responsible for his pain.

"Sorry, can't say I know anything about this man you

seek." She hadn't told a lie. Didn't say she didn't know—just that she couldn't say.

But Joanna's look of disapproval warned Mandy she'd pushed the boundaries of right and wrong.

Austin thanked them for the meal and left the room.

The two sisters grabbed dishes and hurried to the kitchen, where they couldn't be overheard.

"He'll just ask someone else," Joanna warned.

"He won't hear Trace's whereabouts from me." And if she could stop him from searching further, she would. Maybe she could suggest he make inquiries farther north—like the gold fields.

As soon as the dishes were done she hurried outside. Glanced about the cluster of men. Austin went from one to the other, asking questions. If he decided to go up the street...

As if he'd read her mind, he left the men and stepped toward the heart of town.

She hurried after him and fell in at his side. "Seems to me the best place to look for someone would be in the gold fields. People only come here on their way north."

"I'll certainly search there, too. I am determined to find him."

"Why is it so important to you?"

He pondered her question for several steps as she tried to edge him away from the houses and businesses up the street, but he continued doggedly on, peering from one side to the other. "I don't see how it's any of your business." He flicked her a glance. "Ma'am."

"What if I make it my business?"

He snorted. "Why would you?"

She considered her response. "Let's say, just for conversation's sake, that if I happened to know this man you're asking about—"

"Trace Owens."

"Or someone like him. Why would I, or anyone, tell a complete stranger about it? You could be one of those lawless men who wander through town looking for easy gold. They don't mind if they find it by panning or by robbing." Did he understand that she cared about his motive in looking for Trace?

"I don't want his gold or anyone's. I just need to talk to Trace." He slowed his steps enough to glance at Mandy. "We·grew up together. We were great friends."

"*Humph.* Seems if you were great friends you'd know where he was."

"Something happened."

Yeah. You turned out to be a traitor. Played a part in murdering his parents. "I expect it was something awful enough that this man doesn't want to see you again."

Austin stopped so abruptly that Mandy had to backtrack to his side.

"It was something very awful."

"What did you do?" If she heard the story from his lips, perhaps she would get a clue that would help Trace overcome his pain.

Austin sucked in a long breath, let it out in a shudder. "It's a long story. Not sure you want to hear it."

"Try me." They reached Glory's shop. "Why don't we sit a spell, and you can tell me." She indicated the steps at the front door and almost sagged with relief when he sat down. She sat as well.

"I did something unforgivable."

"Is anything ever that bad?" She wanted to hear how he'd justify his actions.

"Unfortunately, yes." He buried his head in his hands.

Mandy felt no sympathy for him. The man deserved every bit of misery he felt.

"I'm from Missouri, as is Trace. The Bushwhackers are a strong bunch in that state. I once thought I agreed with them enough to join their cause, but I discovered I don't like the way they get their point across. I've left the group."

Mandy brushed dust from one pant leg then leaned back on her elbow, observing the man. It was good to hear he might have regrets.

"I need to find Trace and tell him I left them. But there's more." He stared into space. "I was involved in something that hurt Trace. Hurt his sister and his parents. People I love." Slowly, as if he had to force the words from his lips, he told the story that Mandy had already heard. But Austin's version differed.

"I arranged for Trace to be absent so he wouldn't try to stop them. I thought I was doing him a favor. You know, preventing him from trying to defend his family and maybe getting shot. I thought they only meant to force Mr. Owens to provide them with food and supplies. When I heard what they really intended, I tried to warn the Owenses, but two men held me back. By the time I managed to get free, the house was nothing but a pile of ashes. And Trace was threatening to take justice into his own hands. I think the only reason he didn't was because Cora needed him at her bedside."

The story shocked Mandy to the point she couldn't think.

Austin let out a gust as if his lungs hadn't released air for several minutes. "By the time Cora was able to be left alone, the wheels of justice had determined the fire was an accident. They got away with murder. I left and went north, trying to find a place where I could escape the war and my accusing thoughts." Another deep sigh. "Escaping yourself isn't possible. I did a lot of soul searching.

Spent a lot of time on my knees seeking forgiveness. I met a preacher man who assured me God could and would forgive anything. Finally, I found a degree of peace." He rubbed his chest absently.

He'd found the answer to guilt. The same answer must surely apply to hate and unforgiveness. She wanted to grab him and drag him to see Trace this minute. But she still wasn't sure what he wanted.

"So you are wanting to start over again with your friend?"

"I don't know if it's possible. How could he ever forgive me for my part in this? But I need to tell him I'm sorry. I never meant for it to happen. I need to ask his forgiveness." His voice dropped to an agonized whisper. "Even if he's not willing to give it."

Mandy considered her options. Was this an answer to prayer for Trace's healing? If she didn't take the man to see Trace, she faced two possibilities—Austin might find Trace through someone else and go to him, or he might leave on the ferry, and Trace would miss this chance to deal with his problem.

She made up her mind. What better person to help Trace than the man who caused his hurt? "I know Trace."

Austin burst to his feet and faced her. "You know him? Where is he?"

"Come on. I'll take you."

As she led the way, he almost ran over her.

Footsteps approached the camp. They weren't taking any pains to be quiet, which meant they either didn't know someone inhabited this part of the hill, or they knew and had no interest.

Nevertheless, Trace grabbed his rifle and waited.

Several times men had approached but had quickly

departed when they realized Trace wasn't prepared to be welcoming.

Cora didn't head for the tent but pulled on her bonnet as she remained seated on a log. No doubt she expected the men to pass.

Men? He cocked his head. One voice sounded like a woman. In fact, it sounded like Mandy. Was it getting so bad he couldn't hear a woman and not think of her? Yes, it was. If only he could feel free to love her fully.

All his pleading with God for an answer had yielded nothing.

He heard them leave the path and head toward the clearing. He moved forward to meet them.

They stepped away from the trees.

He fell back. Every muscle in his body spasmed with shock. Somehow he found his voice. "Austin. Why are you here?" He half raised his rifle then lowered it. Shooting the man would not ease his anger. "Mandy, why are you with him?"

She signaled the man to hold back and crossed to Trace's side. "He's been looking for you to say he's sorry. You need to hear his side of the story. Hear how God forgave him. He can help you."

Roaring fires of rage seared his veins. "God might forgive him, but I never will. Get out of here. Both of you." He waved the rifle like a club. "I never want to see you again. Either of you."

Austin took a step closer. "Trace, hear me out."

"I'm not interested in anything you have to say. Get out." He drove them away, ignoring Austin's pleading to listen and Mandy's begging eyes. They disappeared through the trees.

"Traitors, both of you," he called after them.

He breathed hard, unable to think beyond the shock

of seeing Austin and the horror of knowing Mandy had brought his enemy right to his new home.

He spun around to face the house. All but finished. But he'd find no peace here now. Mandy's presence would haunt him everywhere he turned. Muttering angry words, he grabbed up the saddle bags. "Start packing."

Cora didn't move.

"Did you hear me? We're leaving. Get your stuff together."

"Trace, you aren't being rational. This is our new home." She nodded toward the house. "We can't leave."

"We'll find somewhere else. Maybe we'll find a place where people aren't traitors."

She still didn't move. "People are the same all over. Sometimes they are evil. Sometimes they simply make mistakes." She rose and crossed to face him squarely, her arms across her chest. "And sometimes they actually want to help. But you have to give them a chance."

"I've given all the chances I intend to give. Pack your things. There's at least three hours before dark. We're going to take advantage of it."

"What if I say I'm not going?"

He stopped his furious stuffing of things into bags. "You think you can manage on your own?"

"I could live at the stopping house."

"And let all those men stare at you?" It was cruel but necessary.

Her face crumpled, but she did not cry. "Trace, you have a problem."

"I'm aware of that." The only solution for it was to move on.

Cora packed reluctantly. He saddled the horses and hung their belongings on each. They mounted and headed for the ferry, arriving in time for the last crossing north.

He expected to put a goodly distance between themselves and Bonners Ferry before he'd find a place to camp for the night.

"Where are we going?" Cora asked, a good deal of exasperation lacing her words.

"Might as well go look for gold."

She harrumphed, a sound so much like their ma used to make that Trace stared.

"You will never find enough gold to replace the friendship and love Mandy offered you."

"I intend to try."

"You'll never succeed." She turned her attention to the cat in her arms, dismissing Trace.

As they rode, he re-lived every minute of the visit from Austin and Mandy. Why had Mandy brought him? Out of malice? He couldn't think so.

Then why?

The answer dawned, slow and certain.

Because she wanted to help him. She thought seeing Austin would serve some good purpose.

He warred with his anger. Only it wasn't fury that caused his stubborn refusal to face the truth. It was pride. He could not let go of his righteous resentment that justice had been denied him…that friends had proven false.

He'd prayed for God to help him. Then Mandy said Austin could help him. Had God sent an answer? But why would He choose Austin—his ex-friend and enemy— to carry a message to him? His conscience asked, Was he willing to listen to Austin if it meant relief from this burning, unyielding hate and unhappiness?

Mandy rushed past the stopping house. She went on until she reached a grassy hillside overlooking the river where there was no traffic.

She threw herself on the grass and pounded the turf till her fists ached. She lay there crumpled for a while, but the tears wouldn't come. At last she sat up and stared at the water gurgling past.

Trace said he never wanted to see her again. He was determined to remain miserable, rejecting every good gift God offered. Wallowing in his hate like a pig in mud. But she couldn't remain angry. Instead, wave after wave of pain and despair washed over her.

She heard Glory approach but didn't bother to look up.

Glory sank to Mandy's side, their arms brushing. "Joanna told me Trace's old friend showed up asking after him. What happened?"

"I took him to see Trace."

Glory waited without comment.

"The man said he'd changed. Said he regretted any part he'd had in what the Bushwhackers had done. He wanted to ask Trace's forgiveness. I thought it would help Trace to talk to him, so I took him to see Trace."

"I'm guessing it didn't go well."

"Trace chased us away. Said he never wanted to see me again." Her voice broke. Her nose stung, and she sniffed. "I always think I can fix things for people. I should let them sort out their own problems."

Glory wrapped her arm around Mandy. "Sweetie, you only want people to be happy. Nothing wrong with that."

"Then why did it turn out so bad?" She rested her head on Glory's shoulder.

"Because you can't force people to change. They have to decide that on their own."

"Then I guess I don't stand a chance with Trace. He's too pigheaded to give up his anger."

"It's a pretty big thing to give up. After all, his parents

were murdered, and no justice was offered. But remember, 'With God all things are possible.' "

"That's what Levi told Trace."

Glory gave a soft laugh. "It's one of his favorite verses."

They sat in contemplative silence for a moment before Mandy spoke again. "What am I supposed to do now? He said to never come back."

"Keep loving him. Keep praying. Don't give up."

It was good advice from a sister who'd kept loving and praying until she and Levi sorted out their problems. "Guess if it worked for you it can't fail for me."

Glory snorted. "You're saying your problems are nothing compared to mine?"

Mandy tried to laugh but couldn't. "If only it were so."

Glory got to her feet and reached down to pull Mandy up. "I don't imagine any of them are big compared to God's power. Now let's get home before Joanna gets really worried."

The next morning, Mandy rose with a plan in mind. She would return to the clearing and act like nothing had happened. If Trace wanted to get rid of her he'd soon discover he would require a lot more than angry words.

Three times on the way up the trail she almost changed her mind, remembering the look on Trace's face when he saw Austin and the way he'd driven them away. But she would not let things between them end in such a fashion. Fact was, she didn't intend to let them end at all.

She stepped into the clearing and halted, waiting for Trace's reaction. Silence. Had he seen her coming and ducked away? Taken Cora with him? "Trace, I'm here."

Nothing. Why, he'd even taken down the tent. Why would he do that?

A dreadful suspicion scratched at her brain. She looked for his horses. Gone. Unless he'd moved them out of sight.

She circled the area. The campfire was cold. No pots or dishes lay about. Perhaps they'd moved into the cabin. But she didn't need to go any farther than the door to see the inside was empty.

She darted around the cabin. No tools. Nothing. She went to her twig house and stepped inside. It, too, was empty.

They were gone.

She returned to the middle of the clearing and turned around twice.

Trace had left. Without good-bye. Without telling her. He couldn't be more obvious that he wanted nothing more to do with her.

She collapsed to her knees. "Oh God, why didn't You stop him?" The words rang with a familiar tune. How often had she called out to God the very same thing when Pa left yet again?

"Oh God, bring him back. Please."

Her voice rang out in the silence. "I'll go after him." But she knew the futility of trying to catch up to a man who didn't want to be found. Pa had taught her that lesson well.

She sank into a ball, her palms on the ground, and groaned. She loved Trace, exasperating as he could be, but when had her love ever been enough?

She knew he loved her, too. But his anger and hate quenched it.

For a long time she didn't move. Barely breathed. Didn't want to feel but couldn't stop the pain any more than she could stop the sun from shining.

Glory's words seemed to echo from a distant place. *"With God all things are possible."*

Was their love possible?

Could she trust God to make it so?

"Who else can I trust?" she whispered. But real trust rested in knowing God would fulfill His promises.

She struggled a moment longer. Trace had every reason in the world to be angry, unwilling to forgive. Only God could show him another way. With bowed head she asked for that to be accomplished.

One thing she knew, besides God's faithfulness. Trace loved her. Surely one day, with God's help, his love would conquer all else and he would return.

Maybe not today. Or tomorrow. Or even next week.

But when he did, he would need a house. She pushed to her feet and faced the log cabin. Only a little left to be done on the roof before it was finished.

When he returned he would find the house ready to live in.

She climbed the ladder to the roof and set to work.

As she hammered, her heart grew calm and steady, knowing God would also be busy doing His work in Trace's heart.

She paused, the hammer suspended midair, and listened. Voices. People were coming. She sank back out of sight on the far side of the roof and waited. Hopefully the strangers would pass on by, because she was in a precarious, vulnerable position.

The sound of horse hooves stopped. She clung to the roof and waited.

But the riders didn't continue. They turned in and came toward the clearing.

"This is home now."

Cora? That was most certainly Cora's voice. Who did she talk to? Dare she hope?

She rose to her knees and stared down at the pair. "Trace?"

He looked up. Saw her there and stared hard. He blinked and stared again. "Mandy, what are you doing on the roof?"

"Trace. Cora." She scrambled down the ladder and ran toward him. "You've come back." Had Trace come back because he loved her? She paused.

But Trace swung off his horse and ran toward her, caught her in his arms and hugged her to his chest. "I had to come back."

"Why?"

Cora dismounted, gathered Goliath in her arms. "Because my big brother can be very smart at times." She headed for the woods.

Mandy leaned back to study Trace's face, her heart clamoring up her throat at the way his eyes shone, his gaze sought hers and clung. "What did she mean?"

"She thinks I've come to the right decision."

Mandy waited.

He led her to one of the logs they used as a bench and pulled her down beside him, never letting her out of his arms. "Remember how I said hate poisoned love?"

She nodded.

"Well, only if I choose to hold on to hate rather than love." He again searched her face, as if he couldn't get enough of it, had forgotten overnight what she looked like. "I figured it made more sense to let it go and choose love." He traced the line of her jaw with his fingertips, sending delicious bubbles of joy through her veins. "Mandy, I choose love because my heart can hold nothing else when I am with you. Oh, don't get me wrong. I'm not saying I'll never get angry."

"Of course not," she murmured. "I get angry, too. You may have noticed."

He smiled and continued. "Or that I won't chafe at the injustice of my parents' murder."

"Nor should you." She struggled to concentrate on what he said. She watched his lips move and wished he would say where she fit into all this.

"Mandy Hamilton, I love you. I want to spend the rest of my days seeing your smile, laughing at your tricks, growing and learning and being a family with you." His smile reached deep into his eyes and even deeper into her heart.

"Glad you finally found some sense." She took a deep breath. "Trace Owens, I love you. I want to spend my days with you, too. I want to be with you through your bad times and your good. I want you to hold my hand when I go through bad times and share my joy when I go through good."

"Mandy, will you marry me?"

"Just name the day."

He didn't. Instead, he cradled her face in his palms and bent to kiss her, a kiss full of promises for sweet tomorrows.

They leaned against the cabin wall, arms wrapped around each other, and talked about the ways God had taught them to trust His promises. And still later, as the sun began to set and they'd discussed plans with Cora, a visitor approached the yard.

Austin stood before Trace. "I won't leave until you hear what I have to say."

Trace nodded, his eyes wary, and invited Austin to sit on the log bench. His posture remained stiff, but he held his tongue and let Austin explain all that happened.

"I'm truly sorry. I never meant any of this to happen. Will you forgive me?"

Mandy held her breath. All her thoughts and prayers, all of Trace's agonizing, had come to this moment.

Trace paused, his throat working, and gave a curt nod. A decisive nod. "I forgive you."

They shook hands; then Austin gripped Trace's shoulder. "Thank you."

"I only regret those responsible weren't brought to justice."

"Perhaps they were." Austin shrugged. "The three leaders were shot in an ambush a few months after you left. The rest of the gang dispersed. I'm sure many of them went South to sign up somewhere. But I'm equally certain many of them disappeared, sick of the life they'd lived."

Trace sucked in air. He pressed his hands to his thighs.

Mandy watched him closely. Would he see this as justice or travesty?

His hands relaxed. His shoulders lowered. "It's relief to know they won't kill anyone else and will meet judgment at God's hands."

Mandy gritted her teeth to stifle her whoop of joy. Grinning, she went to Trace's side.

He pulled her close. "It's time to start over. I've found someone to move on with."

Epilogue

Mandy looked at herself in the mirror and tugged at the neckline of her dress, squirmed inside the sleeves, and stuck a loose hairpin back into place. "I can't imagine what Trace is going to say."

"Probably about the same thing Levi is going to say when he sees me."

Joanna looked from one to the other. "You are both radiant brides. They'll pinch themselves to see if this is real and wonder how two cowboys like themselves ended up with the prettiest girls anywhere around."

Mandy took one more look at herself then stood tall. "He's never seen me in a dress."

Joanna chuckled. "The surprise will do him good." She hugged Mandy, careful not to muss her hair. "You're beautiful." She hugged Glory and repeated the words. "Your dress looks good on you, too."

Cora peeked out the door at the crowd waiting outside of the now-completed mission. "Looks like they're ready. Trace and Levi look so handsome in their black jackets. I can't believe Levi decided against wearing his vest. I hardly recognize him." She laughed. "They look a little nervous."

She pulled the door shut and faced the Hamilton women. "I'm nervous, too. But Austin assures me my scars are hardly visible."

It was the first time Cora would go out in public without some kind of bonnet to hide her face.

Mandy hugged the girl who was about to be her sister-in-law. "He's right, you know. When you smile, no one sees anything but your beauty."

Cora smiled then, proving Mandy's point.

"I expect my business will pick up significantly when people hear I have a pretty young assistant," Joanna said, smiling at her new helper, Cora. "It's time to go."

Cora kissed Mandy's cheek then marched toward her brother.

Mandy held Joanna's elbow on one side, Glory on the other, and they followed. Joanna released Mandy to Trace, then Glory to Levi. Mandy knew this was the plan, but all she saw was Trace…his blue eyes shining with love and joy.

* * * * *